Also by Mary-Keith Dickinson

A Divine Scavenger Hunt
Down to Dust
The Bone Hotel

Scavenging for Diamond Dust is an edited combination
of *A Divine Scavenger Hunt* and *Down to Dust*.

SCAVENGING
For Diamond Dust

Mary-Keith Dickinson

ARCHWAY
PUBLISHING

Archway Publishing books may be ordered through booksellers or by contacting:

Archway Publishing
1663 Liberty Drive
Bloomington, IN 47403
www.archwaypublishing.com
844-669-3957

Because of the dynamic nature of the Internet, any web addresses or
links contained in this book may have changed since publication and
may no longer be valid. The views expressed in this work are solely those
of the author and do not necessarily reflect the views of the publisher,
and the publisher hereby disclaims any responsibility for them.

ISBN: 978-1-6657-2954-3 (sc)
ISBN: 978-1-6657-3003-7 (hc)
ISBN: 978-1-6657-2955-0 (e)

Library of Congress Control Number: 2022916526

Print information available on the last page.

Archway Publishing rev. date: 09/09/2022

For my spiritual tribe, visible and invisible.

PROLOGUE

March 1
Bayport, Texas
Journal Entry

If I write, I will suffer. Even breathing in and out seems painful these days. Keeping a journal is my therapist's idea—a psychologically popular tool meant to encourage self-honesty. Whatever. Personally, I think therapy, at least for me, is a waste of time and money, not to mention a huge threat to the status quo of my carefully guarded secrets. There's a nerve-wracking chance that if I write down what I really feel, my words, like flint striking steel, might ignite the festering fodder shoved into the corners of my mind and burn the last coherent thoughts from my brain.

I haven't kept a journal in years—a masochistic starvation of sorts. I used to write stories about handsome princes and horses with wings as a child, but like many of my creative avenues, reality logjammed my innocence with detour signs and other chunks of horror, choking my dreams with the thorny vines of fear and regret, leading to my dead-end life.

Part of me is desperate to find a cosmic reason for my angst. I'm horrified by my recent failures and can't seem to identify any emotions except hatred and blame. Will this pen release me or just become another metaphorical prick thrusting into my psyche, seeking its own selfish satisfaction?

This Freudian drivel is pitiful. The literary police should arrest me. I knew this would happen. Festering fodder? Phallic imagery? Who am I trying to impress? I'm a college professor, not a sixteen-year-old drama queen.

A student once asked me, "Where does God fit into all this philosophy we are studying?"

Good question. Many people believe there is a benevolent force in the Universe; they claim to see the Truth like a perfect theological donut sitting beside their decaffeinated, part-skimmed mocha latte. Not me. I doubt everything, probably because Jesus does *not* seem to love all the little children in the world. If anything godlike exists, it/they must be on permanent vacation.

I keep screaming inside, *What about me?* Who loves me now? My psychiatrist or the moon-eyed checkout boy at the supermarket? Why are so many of us dying inside, flailing alone in the muck and mire?

Sure, basically I'm just a junk-food eating, spiritually bankrupt, pseudo-intellectual fumbling toward some sort of ecstasy, but I never deserved to be cheated on, lied to, abused, and abandoned. Maybe I'm suffering from something I did in a past life. Bad karma.

ONE

"**A**RE YOU WRITING YOUR MEMOIRS?" THE MIDDLE-AGED bartender in the Tiki Hut Lounge with his greasy Elvis hair and scar-like wrinkles irks me for some reason.

"What kind of a bullshit question is that?" I say, tapping my wedding ring nervously on the edge of the sticky bar. Slamming the journal closed, I can almost see my annoyance rush toward the poor man like an invisible tidal wave. He takes a step back, raising both hands in surrender.

"What's your poison?" he inquires with caution.

I squint at the nametag on his Hawaiian shirt. "Do I look toxic, Stanley, or do you say that to all the girls?" My attempt at cocky self-assurance is failing.

Stanley is silent. Like a professional snake handler, he exhales, slowly assessing my lethality, and then in two graceful movements, he wipes the bar with a wet towel and empties my ashtray. Even though he seems washed-up and desperate, his calloused, liver-spotted hands remind me of a favorite uncle who used to touch my cheek and magically produce a quarter from behind my ear.

"Sorry. I'm being a bitch, and I don't know why." I press my forehead against the heel of my hand, trying to stop the buzzing in my ears. "I'm just not feeling normal ... probably getting a sinus infection."

Stanley glances over his shoulder at a seashell-bedecked nautical gauge on the wall. "Yep, the barometric pressure is low today ... can do a number on you if you're not used to it."

Continuing to compulsively mess with my wedding ring, I wind it past the knuckle and accidentally drop it onto the bar where it rolls toward a sink full of suds. Deftly, Stanley snatches it in midair. Drying the ring slowly, he holds it up to one pale blue eye as if looking out to sea through a miniature telescope.

"How long have you been divorced?" he asks in a gritty voice, making eye contact as he drops the gold band into my open hand.

"Quick hands and psychic too?" Having trouble keeping my voice from quavering, I shove the ring into my pocket and lean back.

"Not psychic, just recognize the symptoms. Can I buy you a drink?'

I refuse to cry.

Stanley takes a wineglass from an overhead rack and buffs it with a clean, dry cloth. Then he places a cocktail napkin in front of me, making sure the square is offset, a diamond pointing toward my heart. I hold my breath.

"Chardonnay?"

The pale gold liquid is already swirling around the glass, drawing me into its familiar vortex. Even though the wine smells sharp and on the cheap side, I want it badly. It would be so easy to let the grapey tang numb me for the rest of my life.

"Wait … My husband thinks I'm a … ex–husband … Oh hell, I'm trying to cut down on my drinking, OK?" I blurt.

Stanley stops pouring. "This is a bar; I just assumed. I'm a stupid old fart."

"No, don't take the glass away. Let me breathe in the aroma and pretend. You wouldn't happen to have any Krispy Kreme donuts behind the bar?"

"No, but I can offer you a Coke chaser."

"Diet, please." Reaching again for my now naked ring finger, I fidget. A bar used to be the environment where I felt the most at home.

"So, Stanley, can I ask you a stupid question?"

"Sure, if you don't mind if I smoke." After checking for other customers who might protest, he taps two Camels out of his pack, offers one to me, and lights them both. "What do you want to know?"

"Are you a drinker?"

"Seriously?" He cackles and coughs. "I'm a bartender. What do you think?" he says, the cigarette dangling from his mouth.

"I'm sorry. Don't know why I asked such a personal question."

He moves the shapely wine glass off the napkin and replaces it with a blunt brown Coke.

I take a swig, wishing that it had the magical ability to take the edge off my social awkwardness. Today it would probably take a quart of Chivas to get me back on track.

"Hey, sorry about before," I say, unable to stop the blush. "Obviously, I'm a bit messed up and suspicious of men right now."

"Don't worry about it." Stanley seems embarrassed too. "Yes, I drink—way too much, in fact. On my day off, I take my boat out to fish with a couple of six-packs but never seem to catch anything before I pass out."

I nod and focus on the beach view. "Nobody gets hurt, and the fish get the day off?"

Stanley laughs and looks at me a bit more closely. "So you quit alcohol? Even beer?" he asks, giving me a curious side-eye.

"Not on purpose. I love to drink; it makes me feel sexy and intelligent—just can't handle the fights, the blackouts, and the hangovers. You know how it is."

Stanley nods several times and compresses his lips until they turn white. "Yeah, whiskey kills the pain, but it can kill everything else too, but don't let some asshole ex drive you back to drinkin'."

"A nasty bit of good advice." I bobble my head in unison with him.

He takes a deep drag off his cigarette and holds the smoke in his lungs for a moment before blowing it forcefully down toward his chest and grinding it out in my ashtray.

"Well, sweetheart, you're plenty sexy. I don't know what happened to your marriage, but your ex was crazy to divorce you." He raises his eyebrows and winks.

"What the hell, Stanley!"

Was that supposed to be a compliment? Is he hitting on me? My guts begin to gurgle, and the buzzing in my ear turns into a high-pitched squeal. Does he think I'm some floozy? I pinch my nose and close my mouth, trying to equalize the pressure in my head.

Why have I come to the Beachcomber Hotel? I'm running away from reality, that's why—I, the seeker, am sprinting in the opposite direction of mental health.

"Hey, are you OK?" Stanley looks worried.

I wave him away, rummage in my backpack for a ten-dollar bill and throw it on the counter while heading for the door.

I stumble past the hotel pool onto deep, dry beach sand, stiff-legged, and lurching like one of the walking dead. What's happening to me? Am I having a brain aneurism? Gulping the moist air, I focus on the horizon, a thin line of sanity smashed between sea and sky. With spring break only one week away, Mother Nature seems to be purging in protest, throwing up clumps of rusty orange seaweed in my path. I can relate.

With tears of shame burning my cheeks, I whisper, "Divorced," and the salty wind snatches the word from my lips, daring me to follow it into despair. The pressure in my head shoots fire down my neck and arms as I walk, the pain morphing into panic. I have come to the end of myself.

Afraid of cutting my bare feet on a broken beer bottle or sharp shell, I tiptoe through the seaweed to a bald section of sand and collapse. How is it possible to be so stupid? I don't know why I'm surprised that my husband cheated on me. I knew his infidelity issues before I married him. Moody and distant looked attractive back then. I guess I thought that after we married, our combined psychological knots would somehow blissfully untangle.

I'm obviously incapable of love. I can already feel myself trudging back to mental prison camp where self-pity is the soup du jour. What is my purpose now? Can I go on living?

I used to have a list, no, more like a lifetime plan full of new frontiers to discover and fantasies destined to come true. I clung fiercely to the idea that angels had tattooed the map to bliss on my sweaty palms with invisible purple ink and that someday I would find an amazing partner to share my adventure.

Never shirking the quest, I tried almost everything once, knocking on every metaphysical door, always sprinting down the road less traveled. If a spiritual book or doctrine crossed my path, I devoured it—would have shredded and smoked it to reveal more secrets.

Each fragment of truth revived me for a moment or even a few years, but I always became hungry again. Recently, something subtle and insidious began rising inside me, infecting my soul. So I married the first man who showed up. That turned out well.

Obviously, I'm not smart enough to crack the grand illusive code of life. I've had no epiphanies on my jeep trail to enlightenment. I dig my toes angrily into the sand. How can so much searching lead to so much anguish? I feel swindled out of an inheritance no one promised me. After embracing all the magical, mystical hoopla, I haven't been able to accomplish anything worthwhile … not really.

Suddenly, it feels as if someone has shoved an ice pick into my ear. I can hardly breathe. The fear of death presses in around my heart, and I wish, for the millionth time, that I could scream at someone in in charge.

"Jesus H. Christ! Make it stop!"

TWO

EVENTUALLY, PRESSING MY EYE SOCKETS AGAINST BENT KNEECAPS alleviates the torturous throbbing behind my eyes. I'm hesitant to move in case the pain and fury returns.

"Do you need some help?"

Someone must have walked up beside me—probably concerned about seeing a young woman alone on an empty beach, moaning and rocking. How mortifying.

Without raising my head, I mumble from the depths of my hair. "I'm OK ... just resting for a minute. You can go on; everything is fine."

"You must be joking."

There is kindness in the voice, but my embarrassment shifts into irritation, and I refuse to look up.

"I'm pretty sure that as long as I keep my clothes on and don't break the law, what I do out here is nobody else's business, now please ..." When I finally lift my head, no one is there.

"You wanted to speak to someone in charge?"

I hear the voice all around me, and yet it seems to be originating somewhere in the center of my head.

"Where ... Who are you?"

"Just one of the Gang. Does it matter?"

"What, like a freaking ghost?"

"Ghost is so cliché. I'm much more than that."

"No, this is a stress-induced hallucination, probably caused by my new antidepressant. I refuse to listen or respond."

"*You aren't crazy.*"

"Right. Says who, a psychotic voice in my head? There is no one on the beach for fifty yards in either direction. I wonder if this is late-onset schizophrenia. I must focus on facts, something real like the waves—random yet constant. I understand random. Random equals my life."

"*I am connected to you.*"

"You mean like ... Wait, stop. I don't need to know who you are! I'm just processing in a new way. No big deal."

"*No big deal, except ...*"

"Except what?"

"*If I were a figment of your stress-induced imagination, you would already know the answer.*"

"I don't want anything to do with God."

"*Interdimensional spirituality is complicated. You'll have to settle for this expression of me right now.*"

"Typical. My life is in the toilet, and I get a supernatural underling."

"*I love that about you.*"

"What?"

"*Even though you suspect that you're having a psychotic break, you aren't afraid to sass back at what the Universe throws your way.*"

"You don't know me. What if I just exorcise your ass right now?"

"*Like a demon? That's not how this works. You can't command your skin to crawl off your body.*"

"Skin crawling ... quite an appropriate description."

"*How is this any different from the journaling you were doing before?*"

"Because journaling is *me* writing down *my* thoughts."

"*Are you sure about that?*"

"Besides, if there is a God, He's a selfish bastard who abandoned me a long time ago."

"*Crisis can rip the veil between worlds.*"

"I'm dying, aren't I?"

"*Dying is a dimension of consciousness but not the only one.*"

"Oh great, that's encouraging. Do I have any say in the matter?"

"All of the choices, actually."

"I'm either talking to myself or sliding slowly into madness."

"What about door number three?"

"Maybe your voice only sounds as if it's separate from me."

"Does that make you feel more in control?"

"Yes … No."

"You have lots of questions, right?"

"My heart won't stop palpitating."

"I'm here …"

"Stop it. I didn't ask for your help. Get the hell out of my head."

"You yell out my name all the time—in traffic, when you have an ear-splitting headache …"

"You're Jesus H. Christ?"

"I am a lot of things."

"This is my worst nightmare—don't you dare try to tangle me up in the religious rubbish of my childhood."

"Truth exists, with or without religious rubbish."

"Don't preach at me. I seek truth for a living."

"I'm the answer to your prayer."

"I don't pray. I visualize, meditate, and occasionally shake my fist at the heavens."

"Speaking of fists, what's that in your hand?"

"This? I don't know—a little rubbery piece of trash I'm fiddling with, so I don't run down the beach screaming."

"Look at it again."

"It's a brown rubber Barbie boot I found in the sand. Satisfied?"

"Say that three times fast."

"Brown rubber Barbie boot, brown blubber … not possible."

"Made you laugh."

"Religion isn't funny."

"I'm not religious."

"More like a ghost or guardian angel?

"Don't you want to know what it's all a-boot?"

"Why am I still talking to you? For all I know, you're a disembodied spirit trying to possess my soul. I should kill myself before this insanity leaks out and someone sees it."

"We can talk about anything you want …"

"Tempting, but must I participate in this last-ditch delusion before I die?"

"Which delusion?"

"That I'm not alone."

"You and Ronny loved playing charades. Let's do that today instead of dying."

"What do you know about my brother Ronny?"

"That boot was made for … Come on, walk this way."

"Should I hunch over and drag one foot?"

"What hump?"

"A *Young Frankenstein* movie reference … Impressive."

"Test me all you want."

"Ghosts don't haunt just anyone—unless you're a brain tumor trying to help me cross over."

"Be still, Hope Delaney."

"A tumor that speaks … and knows my name."

"I find you fascinating."

"That's because I'm dying."

"You have died many deaths."

"What's that supposed to mean?"

"Wouldn't you like to know?"

"Are you a tumor? Just tell me. I can take it."

"What is the real question?"

"Is there meaning to the Universe? Does God, or something like that, really exist?"

"Yes."

"Yes? Just like that?"

"You asked."

"I don't believe you. Love sucks. Couldn't you or one of your gang members have shown up earlier and stopped me from ruining my life?"

"Again, not how it works."

"Am I going to hell?"

"I thought you didn't believe in hell."

"You know what I mean. Secretly, everyone probably believes in hell."

"Let's talk about that."

"Are you the Spirit, from Christianity?"

"You're angry with that version of God. I don't live in a box. I'm here to comfort you … communicate with you, not drag you into a consecrated building."

"So, you aren't God?"

"Let's suspend your incomplete and limiting labels for the time being."

"I don't believe that God talks to just anybody; however, dead people and evil spirits might."

"Fortunately, my multifaceted existence doesn't depend on what you believe."

"I don't want to be friends."

"What if I'm able to meet you exactly where you are?"

"Me, a total fuck up? I'm definitely not one of the chosen few. Besides, you say semi-inappropriate things. Movie stars act more like God than you do."

"Put on your philosophy hat for a moment."

"Nothing about this is logical."

"Just for a few minutes."

"Do I have to?"

"You choose. How's your head feeling?"

"No pain. So what?"

"Nice side effect of our conversation, eh?"

"Way to claim the credit."

"What do you think about DNA?"

"The mystical complexity of DNA is the only reason I can entertain the thought of an intelligent force in the Universe."

"I also happen to know that you're obsessed with metaphysics and other intangible ideas about the soul."

"So you're a mind stalker. What's your point?"

"What if the creative source that is responsible for knitting you together added an individually designed backdoor that leads to a spiritual dimension?"

"I haven't found any backdoors."

"Are you sure?"

"I'll admit that what some scientists call junk DNA *could* hold the answers to every damn thing."

"You won't be sorry."

"Sorry about what?"

"Exploring every damn thing."

THREE

"OK," I continue. "So, if you're so anxious to talk to me, how about telling me what you are, exactly."

"That answer is multifaceted and will take some time."

"Ah, just what I expected, a non-answer."

"Have you ever considered that you and I may have collaborated in creating the current plan for your life?"

"Like before I was born? Why on earth would I *choose* a dysfunctional family and then forget that I had a direct line to God or the angels or whatever you are?"

"A valid question … Let the party begin."

"You know, never mind. I think I'd rather cling to my misery than follow your disembodied voice deeper into insanity; besides, I've broken all ten of your rules."

"Maybe insanity is part of the solution. What if you can finally hear me because you have come to the end of yourself?"

"I didn't say that."

"Did."

"What are we? Preschoolers?"

"You and I are sitting in a mighty big sandbox, and besides, I'm here at your invitation."

"Everyone says Jesus H. Christ. You're lucky I didn't say the f-word."

"Like that would shock me?"

"Besides, I prayed a million prayers when I was young, and no supernatural spirit guide came to save my day."

"You begged God for curly blonde hair. I think you also prayed for your brother to drown in hot lava?"

"You having access to my memories may be the creepiest part of this. Maybe you are a demon."

"Nope."

"That's exactly what a demon would say."

"Your soul was groaning … I responded."

"You make it sound like passing gas."

"Similar …"

"Supernatural beings aren't supposed to say things like that."

"Why not? Farts are funny—on both sides of the veil."

"These are your great words of wisdom?"

"Aren't you looking for proof that I, or 'something like me' exists?"

"Yeah, so, where are the pyrotechnics?"

"Check the seat of your pants."

"Ha-ha, very funny."

"I'm interested in everything you do."

"You act as if we've known each other forever."

"You think; therefore, I Am."

"Not exactly what Descartes said."

"OK. I think; therefore, you are."

"I think (I hear voices); therefore, I am (crazy)."

"You are verbal and intellectual. I'm showing up in this way to make you more comfortable. Every soul is unique. I adapt."

"That idea isn't very religious."

"As I said before, Truth exists, no matter what it's called."

"What if I choose not to believe you?"

"Why should that stop our conversation?"

"You're just trying to flatter me, seduce me into some sick, altered reality because you know how weak I feel right now."

"Hold your face to the sun and let me dry your tears."

FOUR

MY FOURTH-FLOOR CONDO AT THE BEACHCOMBER HOTEL overlooks a Texas-shaped pool flanked on one side by the Tiki Hut Lounge. The sunset fills my view, reflecting light through an assortment of miniature liquor bottles that I have lined up on the balcony railing. Amber, clear, amber, clear—still full, they sing to me. I deserve a drink, don't I? Especially if I'm losing my mind.

Why is it that after touting myself as an ardent seeker of the *otherworldly*, when something or someone weird appears, I immediately interpret the experience as brain damage? That brown rubber Barbie boot just kicked my uptight ass.

What if everything I know about life, history, and my soul is only a vague outline pointing toward something much more amazing? I better not get my hopes up. If I continue to expect nothing, I won't be disappointed.

I would love to savor a couple of these tiny bottles of liquid relief and then go out for some steamed crab legs, drive back to Austin, and quit my job. To be honest, I'm not sure I have much to offer anymore—now that my personal life is in shambles and my perception of reality is blown to bits.

The idea of returning to a classroom of entitled and shiny-faced freshmen makes my guts rumble. Sometimes I feel as if college students are slightly alien—children of the genetically mutated corn with their eyes glazed and empty, reflecting the blue-lighted rectangles of cell phones and laptops. Terrifying.

I return my fond gaze to my faithful friends, Johnnie Walker, Jack Daniels, and Jose Cuervo ... I'm a hussy for these guys. They would never divorce me. Even now, they wait, patiently, suave, or sleazy. I'm not picky. I know just how it will feel when I take them in ... a slow burn, the pleasurable warmth spreading slowly outward, melting the steel bands around my chest.

Drinking alcohol has been my only consistent comfort, my social identity, and my saving grace. How can I give it up forever? I've been much more committed to booze than I ever was to my marriage, but both have ended in spectacular failure. Granted, the romance part of my relationship with alcohol is over—unless I take the "till death do us part" seriously.

If that stupid cop hadn't stopped me while driving home after happy hour—just one unlucky night ... except for that other time, wait ... two other times. I don't think I'm an alcoholic. I do drink *alcoholically* at times. Last week I completed my mandatory AA meetings—ninety meetings in ninety days. I should be OK now, right?

Here's the thing. There seems to be a vast chasm between ninety days of going to court-ordered AA meetings and the ninety-first day. If I go to another meeting, am I admitting to something that isn't true? What if I drink all these little bottles and the voice in my head gets louder or, worse, disappears? Is that what I want? If I'm dying of a brain tumor, communicating with a benevolent spirit from another dimension isn't so bad ... might even be classified as some sort of religious epiphany.

Shit ...

FIVE

THE AA MEETING IS ALMOST IMPOSSIBLE TO FIND. I DON'T WANT to go, but I'm jumping out of my skin. Where do normal people run when they get the heebie-jeebies? Oh yes, they go to a bar and get f-ing drunk! I hate my life.

Worship by the Sea Holiness Church is not much more than a metal building wedged between an acre of storage units and the Island Electric Company. I suppose I should be grateful that almost every city in the United States has a twelve-step group of some kind. Whoopee. Why are so many meetings inside a church? An insidious plot …

Church has never been a safe place for me. For years my father forced me to go to Sunday school and act like a good girl—smile and pretend that the way he treated me at home in the dark was normal. Die, hypocrites, *die!* Jeez! Where did that come from?

Even over the roar of the car air conditioner, I can hear the people inside singing. Must be the end of a regular service. I hate that. They don't sing in AA, thank God. I just realized that I *do* say, *God* quite a bit … unconsciously, of course. Do those ancient names have some sort of cosmic power? Enough to summon my talking tumor?

What am I afraid of? I'm tough, a scrapper. Growing up hard didn't kill me; I learned to survive. I'm not ready to die, but what do I have to live for?

These are good questions for me to ponder … then again, maybe not. I feel a ripple on the dark pond of my mind. Jumping out of the car, I slam the door just in case anything spooky is trying to come through.

"Excuse me, ma'am." I almost touch the arm of a woman with a beautiful profile fanning her face with a yellow hat as she leaves the building. "Do you know if there's going to be an AA meeting in there?"

With one hand on her ample hip, the woman checks out my wind-blown hair, loose-fitting sundress, and flip-flops. I sense that she is looking for something. Not finding it, she resumes her fanning and speaks over her shoulder.

"There better be somethin' happening in there. This heat makes me want to get drunk and kill somebody."

The woman's companion is tall and skinny. His yellow tie matches her hat, and his brown, bald head glistens with perspiration. His smile is a beautiful event.

"Now, Rose," he says patiently. "Don't talk that way. You'll scare the woman. The meeting is around back, young lady, but it's nonsmokin', so we usually do our business here in the parking lot."

"Business?" I ask.

"Do you smoke?" The woman lifts her chin and looks down her nose, challenging me.

"Sure, but I'm out. Can I bum one of yours?"

The three of us lean against my car, puffing silently like awkward teenagers. My arm looks pale and sickly next to her beautiful brown skin.

"Rose is new to the program." The man pats her, and she jerks away. He continues, undaunted. "How many days do you have now, honey?"

"I have four days, old fool—one more day than yesterday when I had three." Her hands are shaking. She braces them against the car and turns to glare at me. "He's been dragging me to church and AA meetings so much I don't have time to pee, much less have a drink."

I'm afraid to speak.

Rose sucks on her long, thin cigarette like a drowning woman might draw air through a straw. Her whole body seems drenched with suppressed rage. Like a moth to flame, I move closer.

"You know, I don't see what God has to do with anything," Rose says while crushing her cigarette butt into the concrete with the pointed toe of a worn-out high-heeled pump. "Slim, I need another one."

Slim patiently taps a fresh cigarette out for her and then lights it.

"I mean, where was God in the back woods of East Texas? He never did me any favors, I'll tell you that right now. They say God's gonna restore me to sanity?" Rose rocks her head from side to side and wags a finger. "I don't think so! Everything would be alright if I could just have a few rum and Cokes."

"Would it?" I ask.

"What did you say, girl?" Rose delivers each word as if there is a fist behind it.

"You're lucky this man here is taking care of you, making you go to meetings. My man dumped me."

I feel like fainting from a sudden adrenaline surge and brace myself in case the woman slaps me.

"Aw, you want me to cry for you? Next you're gonna tell me God loves me."

"I'm not sure I believe in God," I whisper.

Positive this is some huge AA boo-boo, I scramble. "Don't listen to me. I came to these meetings because of a DUI. What do I know?"

As I open my purse and fumble for my keys to make a quick getaway, the woman's face crumbles.

Rose sobs. "You're right. I am lucky, and I really don't wanna drink anymore. There's a hole in my middle. I've poured gallons of rum in that hole tryin' to fill it up—tryin' to forget all that's happened to me."

Slim hands her a handkerchief, and she blows her nose.

"The rum stopped workin', and I got mean. Tell 'er, Slim. Wasn't I mean?"

Slim looks at me, his eyes wide, head nodding.

Suddenly, the woman pulls me into a damp bear hug. She smells like Jasmine, and her large arms are soft. "I'm sorry. You're a good girl. I can tell."

Rose smooths my hair down. "You're brave. You stood up to me. Not everyone does." Rose looks at Slim and smiles. A tiny flash of something jumps between the two sets of coffee-colored eyes.

Slim takes Rose's hand. "We better go in now, honey. The meeting has probably started."

I don't know what to do. Real people don't act this way. The situation feels surreal, like a play. I feel the need to run away and cry.

When I don't follow them, Rose turns and sashays back toward me. "Look at me," she commands.

I make myself meet her gaze, tears filling my eyes. For an instant, I let her in, just long enough for her to see my pain. Satisfied, she tucks my arm under hers and pulls me along beside Slim who places his hand on my other shoulder.

"Well, if the three of us are gonna walk in there like an damn Oreo cookie, you better tell us your name." Rose grins.

I curse under my breath. "Hope." I sigh.

Rose lets out a belly laugh. "Your name is Hope? Did you hear that, Slim? We're bringin' Hope to our meeting!"

SIX

March 2
Journal Entry

YESTERDAY WAS WEIRD ... THAT'S ALL I'LL COMMIT TO SAYING. I claim my right to remain silent because this new development, sure as shit, could be used against me ...

⸺

I like the way my bare heels pound the hard, wet sand at the water's edge. Even sleep-deprived, I feel a bit lighter this morning—not happy, but less extreme. Should I trust this? *Thump, thump, thump*—my thoughts align despite my fears.

"How did you sleep?"

"I was wondering if you'd show up again."

"Check it out! Today when I speak inside her head, she doesn't even hesitate to answer."

"I've decided to have an open mind. Besides, crazy people don't usually contemplate their insanity. You're a stimulating diversion—something new—and I'm curious."

"I've been called worse."

"What do you want from me?"

"This."

"I'll tell you up front. I'm not interested in joining a cult or following religious rules of any kind. I don't want to save souls or participate in ancient rituals. Not my thing ..."

"You helped Rose last night."

"By telling her I don't believe in God? How can doubting your existence be helpful?"

"Whatever you think happened, it was a breakthrough for her."

"The whole encounter was bizarre ... unnatural."

"Sensing my vibe?"

"You wish."

"Everyone doubts what they can't see."

"Sure, whatever."

"I should warn you, though."

"About what?"

"Spending time with me changes things."

"I didn't ask you to show up, and I don't appreciate you using me to do your dirty work, AA or otherwise."

"Right ... I forgot that you have so many other important things to do."

"I claim spiritual progress, not perfection."

"You don't like helping people?"

"Of course, I'm a teacher, remember, and I often lend a hand to others less fortunate than myself."

"What about helping yourself or others like you?"

"They don't need my help, and I'll survive."

"You sound very sure of yourself ..."

"Oh, look what I found!"

"What?"

"You don't know what I'm holding? So much for omnipotence."

"I'm pretending to be trapped in your third dimension."

"How many dimensions are there?"

"First, tell me what you found."

"Here's a hint: it's round and fits in the palm of my hand."

"A fifteenth-century Spanish doubloon?"

"That was mean. I've always wanted to find one of those!"

"What if ... No, never mind."

"You're manipulating me."

"Do you believe in coincidences?"

"Right now, all of my beliefs are in the crapper."

"Do you like it?"

"What? This round piece of green frosted beach glass?"

"That's the one ..."

"If you really knew me—"

"Yes ... Nailed it!"

"Stop. You're embarrassing yourself."

"Why? Because I know you are an avid beachcomber with a penchant for unusual specimens of beach glass?"

"You expect me to believe that the Universe follows me around planting treasures for me to stumble upon? Not buyin' it."

"Describe the glass."

"Totally opaque—smooth but has part of a raised design with letters worn to nubs."

"If this is a random find, tell me a story about how it got here."

"That's stupid. I don't do that anymore."

"Storytelling builds rapport with your audience."

"I'll give you a story—not because you asked me but because I need the practice."

"It's green. Do you think it was a Coke bottle?"

"Shut it!" I snap. "Do you want my story or not?"

"So cranky ..."

"Whose fault is that do you suppose?"

"I didn't make you watch Law and Order *reruns all night."*

"OK fine ... at some point this Coke bottle was broken. Can we agree on that?"

"Maybe an underage fisherman used it to christen his boat?"

"Or possibly, in a fit of rage, that young fisherman hit his brother over the head because he was always interrupting him!"

"Sorry ... I am riveted."

"Thrown into the fathomless deep, the pieces of our poor soda bottle were scattered by random tides to the ends of the earth. For weeks, months, years, the sea pummeled this very shard until all its sharp edges and shiny surfaces were obliterated. Then, a shark inadvertently gobbled it up, along with a small squid, and it was eventually pooped—"

"Remind me to tell you something when you're finished."

"Being supernatural doesn't give you a right to rudeness."

"Very true. Continue."

"Then, as gods are wont to do, you manipulated me and everything else to suit you, finally depositing this glass on the beach so I could pick it up and wax poetic about the meaning of life."

"And the moral of your story?"

"After life breaks your heart and you are thrown overboard, you must survive eons of torture. Then, when your identity is destroyed and you've completely lost your edge, you can look forward to knowing that nothing really mattered anyway because your perception of reality is distorted, and you have no control over what comes next. Class dismissed."

"Yikes. Frightening yet appropriate, according to your way of thinking."

"What do you mean, appropriate?"

"Think of yourself—your life—as a billion-piece jigsaw puzzle."

"I'd hate to imagine the picture on the box. Bet I look fat."

"You try to place each puzzle piece end to end along a single timeline that stretches from the beginning to the end."

"How do you know how I view …? Oh, never mind."

"What if, like the whole puzzle, your past, present, and future all exist at the same time—even if you don't know how the pieces fit yet?"

"What have you been smokin'?"

"My thoughts are medical-grade."

"Not going to touch that."

"Just keeping you on your toes."

"What does beach glass have to with timeless puzzle pieces? I could have easily walked right past your so-called treasure and missed this lovely lesson altogether."

"The glass, Rose and Slim, and the recent events in your life all have the potential to be points of contact with my dimension. Unraveling the secrets of the Universe is not dependent on linear time. All is accessible in this moment."

"Hang on, Mr. New Age …"

"Too much too fast?"

"You don't have to insult me, I get it … *The moment* can be a doorway of sorts. Sounds like Buddha stuff."

"One of my BFFs."

"What was so important that you interrupted my story?"

"I want you to write all of this down."

"Why would I want anyone else to know that I have a talking tumor?"

"People are curious about such things."

"I told you. I'm not religious."

"I know exactly who you are."

"In fact, this whole experience is embarrassing, like I have an unsightly rip in my space-time continuum."

"If I'm not a tumor, what do you think is happening?"

"I guess I'm so depressed that I've created a pseudospiritual experience—answering myself as something wise and godlike."

"So close to the truth … Don't you think that I, the great and powerful Oz-God, might be able to use this so-called imaginary conversation in a positive, growth inducing way?"

"Oz-God?"

"Has a ring to it … I Am the one behind the curtain."

"It's better than Casper. Wait, the man behind the curtain was just a human trying to make the best out of being blown off course. Shouldn't that be me?"

"Nice catch. Your perception of God is a big scary projection made up of false beliefs that elicit fear and sacrifice."

"You're right in many ways. I guess Oz-God is a good place to start. Humpty Dumpty might work, but the metaphor of breaking with no hope of getting my shit together is depressing."

"Crisis does crack the egg open."

"Humpty Dumpty or Oz-God, your turn to choose."

"Now who's the comedian?"

"I don't think pious people like it when you show up to an *undesirable* like me."

"Pious people can be very invested in hiding their mistakes."

"You're right. Those of us who have made large and public blunders have less to lose. My pride gets slammed all the time."

"Explain …"

"Just when I think I have a handle on things—*bam*—something shameful happens!"

"Your perceived failure has made the veil between us thinner."

"And if I'm subconsciously making up this conversation?"

"You are making it up."

"What the hell?"

"You are interpreting what is happening—working with me to create a new reality."

"So, none of this is *really* real?

"Define real."

"True, factual, tangible, and perceptible."

"Is it real to you?"

"What's real for me may not be real for anyone else. Why are you messing with my head?"

"Exactly. Truth is Truth no matter whose mouth it comes out of."

"But what if they're wrong?"

"That's a conversation for another day."

"Many intellectuals think religious people are ignorant."

"Do they think Buddhists are dumb?"

"Buddhism is usually considered cool."

"Are Hindus stupid?"

"You think I'm prejudiced against Christians."

"You can become stuck in places of pain and rejection. Until you can understand the issues you were born into, the truth can remain elusive … no matter what you believe."

"So, if I were born into a Muslim family?"

"Same process applies. Define your box and the lessons you chose. Begin where you are … Nothing about the who, what, and where of your birth is random, remember?"

"Care to elaborate?"

"If you try to skip over the process or deny your past lessons without knowing their purpose in your life—"

"Don't tell me. I will just re-create the same situations over and over till I get it?"

"Such a quick study."

"Or I could choose not to believe or analyze any of this at all?"

"You could, yes."

"But …?"

"Rebellion, self-pity, and bitterness might remain your best buddies."

"Buzz kill!"

"Transformation and enlightenment are always a choice, but processing like this might pull you back from the edge."

"I am *not* on the edge."

"Afraid you'll be bored?"

"Uh … no."

SEVEN

"YOU ALWAYS DID LOOK DELICIOUS IN A BIKINI."

I hear Steve's voice from far away ... some distant universe, a demonic place where gargoyles leer and dragons eat fair maidens. With my eyes still closed, I smell scotch, hear ice tinkling, and catch the squeak of plastic as he arranges his body on the lounge chair next to mine.

Here in the land of sunny poolside napping, my ex-husband is an unwelcome abomination. If I don't acknowledge his presence, does he really exist? Which philosopher proposes that? How quickly I forget. That's all right; I *want* to forget.

"What are you doing here, Steve?"

"Sweetheart, don't be mad. I was worried about you now that everything is final."

I can feel the familiar, poison-laced adrenaline shoot through me, turning my heart to stone—the alchemy of survival kicking in.

"You no longer have the right to stalk me." I count the heartbeats pounding in my ears.

"None of your friends knew where you were, so out of desperation I called your therapist."

"What?" I bolt upright, immediately grabbing a towel to shield my breasts from his proprietary ogling. "How dare you!"

His subtle smile makes me want to vomit. This is exactly the reaction that turns him on, and I fell for it—again. I hate him so much.

"Now wait a minute, Hope. You've been refusing to return my calls, and you could be suicidal. I'm only thinking of you."

"Don't flatter yourself, Steve. I no longer have to answer your calls. That's what divorce means. If you need something, talk to my lawyer."

I'm baffled by my ignorance. Why couldn't I see what a predator this man is? I suppose a victim-shaped socket is always looking for an abusive plug. Yuck—not the image I want in my head right now.

"In all honesty, it wasn't your shrink who said you might be at the beach; it was her secretary." Steve reaches toward my arm, moving his finger an inch away from my skin, moving from shoulder to elbow without touching me. I feel defiled anyway and pull farther away.

"Are you banging the secretary too? Speaking of sleazy, where *is* your new girlfriend? Did she come with you, or is she sick of your shit already?"

Steve looks off into the distance as if my words have wounded him. I know better.

"I can see why you might resent me, Hope, we've both made some mistakes. I wanted ours to be an amicable divorce but …"

This is old territory. I don't have to play anymore. I am no longer his wife. He just wants me to know he can find me—that he still has enough power to infiltrate my therapist's office. I change tracks.

"Listen, Steve, I don't care how you tracked me down. I don't care who you are screwing, and I'm not suicidal so you can leave."

I send him a castrating look over the tops of my sunglasses. He is tan, and his emerald-colored eyes are bright and dancing to the whiskey tune. I married this man for his looks. I forced all his weaknesses into a cheap Tupperware container and tucked it into a Deepfreeze so I could make myself his chattel—another humiliating revelation.

He catches me staring at him and shifts his body slightly so his tan biceps glisten in the sun.

"For God's sake, Steve, stop flexing. Why are you here?"

"OK, calm down. I know you're still raw and hurting, so I'll leave. We are going back tonight anyway."

"We? Oh, forget it." I lie down and put my sunglasses back on.

"By the way," he continues, "remember when my mother gave you her locket? She never believed we would break up."

But the shrew prayed for it daily, I think to myself. "I don't know where the hideous thing is. Sorry."

He suddenly encircles my wrist with his oily fingers.

"Don't touch me," I growl, trying to keep the nearby sunbathers from looking at us.

Instead of letting me go, his grip tightens enough to bruise, but I make no sound. "Have you forgotten that there isn't one inch of your body that doesn't have my permanent fingerprints on it?" His smile takes on a hard false edge. "My mother wants the locket back. Since you and I never had any children, she is hoping to give it to—"

"You got that slut pregnant? You ... you ... monstrous fuck!"

He releases my wrist and runs his fingers through his thick hair, as if relishing the idea of being a father.

"You hate kids ... Your sleazebag has no idea, does she?"

"Hope, don't be so bitter. You could at least call Angela by her name. Don't forget that I was very generous to you regarding our divorce settlement, and I'm only asking you for this one thing."

"Shove it, Steve."

He laughs as if I've said something funny.

I feel myself morphing into a diabolical fiend with six-inch talons—a skull-shattering screech crawls up my fire-singed throat ...

"Is everything OK here?" Bartender Stanley has come to my rescue. He must have been watching us from the Tiki Hut. In an instant, all my uncharitable thoughts about the bartender disappear. Steve could take him out with one punch, but he won't.

"Thank you, Stanley. This man means nothing to me." I gather my things with shaking hands and take Stanley's arm, turning my back on the wreckage of my past.

EIGHT

WHAT AN ARROGANT JERK. STEVE DELANEY IS ALL THE PROOF I need that some humans evolved from a lower life form ... like a fluke or shit-eating cryptosporidium.

I must breathe and try to clear my mind. Surely this isn't how men and women were meant to treat each other. At this point, I can't see myself ever finding the kind of relationship I've dreamed about; my man-picker is broken.

I keep coming back to Oz-God's image of the puzzle pieces and how many of mine have men's faces on them. I can barely tolerate the idea that my disastrous marriage could be part of a preordained Plan that I helped create. Martyrdom and victimhood are much more satisfying than taking responsibility for my choices.

After a dinner of a dozen raw oysters and two virgin piña coladas, I should be rejuvenated; instead, my inner landscape feels apocalyptic. For the first time, I want Oz-God's voice but hear nothing—only the rhythm of the waves. I imagine Steve's flashing white shark teeth ...

The beach is almost abandoned. As I walk along the surf's edge, twilight has turned into near darkness. The quarter moon and stars are blurry behind thick, humid air. There are no cars now, and only a few indistinct figures roam near the dunes. Should I be afraid? Why can't I walk alone at night without worrying about getting raped—or worse?

Someone is moving about fifty feet to the right of me, matching my pace. I saw the flash of a penlight a moment ago. When I speed up, so do they. Steve could have followed me from the hotel, tracking me like prey until I was alone and vulnerable. Is he capable of hurting me in a permanent way?

Damn it! What if it isn't Steve but some random psycho who crouches in the dunes at night, waiting for stupid bitches like me? Stupid! Stupid!

Wait … What the hell am I saying? I'm not stupid. It's only nine o'clock. I'm sober and fully dressed. It shouldn't matter what I'm wearing, and yet, it does … such a paradox.

The days of silent victimhood are shifting for women, but that doesn't change the fact that many men are still wired differently from us. A woman in a tight, short dress and high heels with her boobs hanging out can still elicit what I like to call the *Playboy* magazine response.

It's kind of cruel for women to pretend this doesn't happen. I don't know if it is something cultural or a product of my past, but I was programmed to seduce or become a victim—nothing in between. Once I snare a man long enough to gather a few dates together, my emotions usually shift, and the rules change. I begin accusing him of being a sex addict and not interested in my mind. If he reacts with anger and threatens to break up with me, my behavior flips again, and I will go to any lengths to win him back—even if it means marrying him.

I don't think I'll be writing any of this part down. I support and believe that women need to speak up about being abused, but I'm messed up too. Who wants to admit that?

In my defense, I've had seasons in my life where I hid my body behind loose clothing, didn't wear makeup, and focused on sharing my soul during deep and intellectual conversations with men. They were often gay, however.

For me, the relationship game doesn't seem to be about looks or even sexual orientation but control. If I were a man, I would hate women. We tantalize and test them, basically demanding that they do everything our way—one minute I'm hot after his body, and the next I'm nonresponsive and crying like a needy little girl.

In a relationship like Steve's and mine, nobody's needs were met, and we both took our sexuality underground—looking for someone else or the impersonal release provided by the Nora Roberts soft-porn club.

Has that shadow man moved closer to me, or did I imagine it? I'm too far away from the hotel to outrun anyone. In case these are the last moments before my grisly murder, I stop walking and listen to the waves … My breath is shallow and ragged. The shadowy figure turns and walks toward me, but I can't see any facial features or clothing details that I could report to police later—only that it's a man, and he's huge. I freeze. His intent is obvious, and I am paralyzed by memories from long ago. If I faint, maybe I won't feel any pain …

NINE

"*Y*OU'RE BLEEDING."

"Where?"

"*Inside.*"

"So, Oz-God, did you enjoy my paranoid freak-out just now?"

"*I never enjoy misery.*"

"Do we have to talk about it?"

"*No.*"

"Don't laugh, but I'm actually glad to hear from you. Things aren't going too well."

"*I noticed.*"

"I don't know what to say. The dune lurker didn't want to rape or kill. He was actually worried someone else might hurt me and said he was keeping an eye on me while I walked alone on the beach."

"*A lot of your past trauma seems to be bubbling to the surface.*"

"Seeing Steve didn't help."

"*Is there something specific you want to talk about?*"

"I feel small, weak, and out of control. I have nothing intelligent to articulate."

"*Articulate is a very intelligent word.*"

"Stop patronizing me."

"*I've noticed that lack of control makes you cross.*"

"You should be used to it by now."

"*What else are you worried about?*"

"You, manipulating me."

"*Is this about one of your past experiences with organized religion?*"

"You're in the same gang or astral plane with God the Father, right? I know all about the horrors that fathers can inflict. Just like Rose, I have an aching pit inside me, so deep that nothing can heal it. I've tried to get past it, but my anguish is too pervasive. Now please leave me alone."

"Really?"

"No, don't go. I just want to be free."

"Free to …?"

"To make my own decisions. I've lived under one tyrant or another my whole life. Now when I finally pull away from Steve, you show up."

"Another tyrant?"

"If the wrathful robe fits …"

"Would you like to move our conversation inside? You're shivering."

"What are you, my date?"

"Maybe."

"That's hysterical."

"Ours is a sacred romance."

"Please, I've had enough creepiness for one evening."

"Yes, you have."

"I don't want to talk about who you are, tyrants, or any of this crap. Religion is a myth, damn it! No belief system has a corner on the market. Don't you know how many cultures have an Adam-and-Eve-type creation story or a Great Flood?"

"Let's jump off this cliff together."

"Won't you just answer my questions without the drama?"

"I mean you no harm, Hope Delaney …"

"I'm confused, and it makes me want to get drunk."

"OK, we'll play school. Remember that game?"

"Poor Ronny. I used to make him wear a dunce cap and stand in the corner of the garage."

"No shaming in my classroom."

"Do I have to sit still during your lecture?"

"Sacred myths are universal because they transcend time and give meaning to life, helping the human mind process things like death, love, and suffering."

"I can't believe in a God who punishes, judges, and rejects."

"Neither can I."

"Then what's your purpose here?"

"Loving, connecting, enlightening ..."

"There's got to be an angle," I prod.

"No angle. That's always been the Plan. There have been deviations ..."

"So, you agree?"

"With what?"

"The Creation story is a myth?"

"As you pointed out, the fact that unrelated cultures across time and geography have similar creation traditions bolsters a myth's credibility, don't you think?"

"I'll tell you what really sets me off. How can religious fundamentalists say every word in the Bible is factual?"

"Tell me how you really feel."

"I suppose there are prophecies and parables that teach simple universal lessons about living life on Earth. But I think there are many holy writings that have truth to offer."

"I agree."

"Another surprising statement from you."

"Free your mind."

"Which direction? Forward or backward?"

"The flip side of myth or Mythos is Logos."

"Give me a second. Let me look at my cheat sheet. Ah yes, Google says lowercase *logos* comes from the Greek and means 'logic.' When capitalized, *Logos* means 'the Word of God, or the principles of divine reason, and creative order, usually associated with Jesus Christ.' Oh brother ..."

"Why does that irritate you?"

"I don't like talking about Jesus."

"Mohammed and Gautama Buddha too, or just Jesus?"

"Can we stop now?"

"Are you afraid I'm trying to trick you?"

"I just don't see the point of debating beliefs that are ancient history."

"You teach philosophy. I thought you liked arguing."

"Very funny. For me, Jesus goes into the myth box, not the box of reason and order."

"Mythos and Logos are simply two aspects of Truth."

"Here's a question for you … Am I a product of random selection?"

"In the beginning, God created the heavens and the earth. Such a great line, don't you think … so simple and to the point."

"Which is more powerful, myth or reason?"

"If I said both?"

"Seriously, a six-day creation? That concept has very little to back it up. I've been to the Grand Canyon and the arches at Moab. Erosion is a very slow process. It probably took a few billion years just for Earth's crust to stop shifting around. Believing that a myth is factual is just dumb and unenlightened."

"Focusing on Genesis, or any religious metaphor, as fact is the least productive way to look at it."

"Then why take any of it seriously?"

"What would you tell a four-year-old who asks where babies come from?"

"Mommy's tummy, of course."

"But how does the baby get in there?"

"The daddy plants a seed inside the mommy, and it grows into a baby."

"Is that a fact?"

"All right, point taken. The use of stories and metaphor could be a way to simplify and present reality to primitive humans."

"Does that make the stories a lie?"

"I suppose not, but I want more facts—something I can depend on."

"Facts change. Earth used to drop off into nothingness, according to the facts."

"I understand what you're saying, but …"

"Earthlings have limitations, and metaphoric teaching works. It takes what is unknowable and associates it with concepts that can be understood within a specific time period."

"But we aren't primitive now."

"If you only knew ..."

"That's just it. I *want* to know. What about time travel and quantum entanglement?"

"Linear time as you know it now is relative to space, distance, gravity, and a few other quantum things that I won't bore you with."

"Are there dimensions in which time ceases to exist?"

"Time is a three-dimensional Earth construct created for learning and to help keep the more primitive parts of the human brain from imploding."

"You speak as if there are other inhabited planets."

"Let's focus."

"You're right. My fragile mind is spinning."

"The Truth is out there."

"Why are you only talking about the Bible? I detect religious preference here ..."

"You're an American and come from a Judeo-Christian heritage. These are the stories that apply to your specific cultural experience. If you had grown up as an atheist or a Hindu, I would be utilizing other source material right now."

"Is this how you approach everyone?"

"I know your issues and the way your mind works."

"OK, fine! Since we are barking up my childhood belief tree, what about Adam and Eve? What's that metaphor about?"

"Adam was representative of the best design of a human prototypes perfected over time ... a lot of time."

"You said *perfected*, so we did evolve!"

"God as a creator being activated certain parts of this chosen prototype's DNA, fused a couple of chromosomes together, and added a bit of this and that from here and there, which made Adam different—special."

"Then after breathing some magic Logos into his mouth ... abracadabra—a new spirit-human species?

"Something like that."

"What are you leaving out?"

"Baby steps, Hope."

"Your description kind of knocks a couple of holes in Darwin's theory."

"You're right. Human beings have gone through a process of evolution. It just wasn't as random as Darwin suggested."

"And I thought it was aliens who seeded Earth!"

"If they did, the creation of the first Spiritual Beings on any planet would have been basically the same. There is, after all, only one Source God in the Universe."

"I was just being glib."

"Out of chaos comes order."

"Are you referring to me?"

"Hurricane Hope?"

"OK, Oz-God … Back off."

"When I say Creator of the Universe, what comes to mind?"

"Something infinitely large."

"Don't forget, also infinitely small—the key word being infinite. Everything you know is miniscule when applied to the big picture. The small is a fractal of all that is and there are infinite levels of creation between."

"I'll admit. That's mind-boggling,"

"What is the actual linear distance from your nose to a single neuron firing in your brain?"

"A couple of inches?"

"If the neuron were conscious, would the distance seem the same as it does to you?"

"My nose would be in a galaxy far, far away."

"Exactly."

"What do you mean by fractal?"

"Say you have a dictionary filled with every word ever spoken."

"OK …"

"Now put that dictionary into a leaf shredder. What do you get?"

"A mountain of intelligent mulch?"

"The mulch is made up of bits of the original. If each tiny piece had within its atomic structure the power to reproduce the entire book, it would represent a fractal of the whole."

"Why did you show up in my life right now—aside from trying to bring order to my chaos?"

"I love you. We have always been connected."

"Are you trying to say I am a fractal of God? That's bullshit."

"Why does that idea scare you so much?"

"I feel invaded, like I no longer have the choice to ignore your confusing ethereal world."

"Having no choice is slavery. I'm not into that."

"Your words annoy me."

"OK, here is a more philosophical word—Dualism."

"Do you mean mind versus matter?"

"Black versus white, good versus evil … Any pair of opposites will suffice."

"Go on."

"Free will means you can choose either polarity or hang out in the gray area in between. There are lessons to be learned at every point along the continuum."

"Free will is a part of our original DNA, right?"

"What if in the beginning good and evil were not originally separated into polar opposites?"

"Then no one would know what is right or wrong."

"Aha! The plot thickens …"

"I see. Right and wrong differ according to culture, religion, politics, etc."

"Yes, but all choices can lead to soul learning … whether they are perceived as right or wrong."

"Talk about chaos! That must be why you created religion … to tell us what to do?"

"I didn't create religion. I created the Garden, a 'neighborhood' big enough to include everyone and all their lessons."

"I always look for ways to skip the steps."

"Evolution happens over time. You can't cheat the system without delaying the process."

"But it's your fault! Free will *makes* us cheat!"

"*Why do you say that?*"

"Obviously, I don't know what's best for me. My decisions seem logical at the time but usually turn to crap."

"*Free will is tied to the human ego. The ego wants to be God and have godlike knowledge of good and evil.*"

"Can't we stop with the Garden myth?"

"*It's a great metaphor, what can I say?*"

"Our prototypes made one bad choice, and now we're all out on our collective asses? Pretty harsh."

"*Having free will makes it more difficult to find your way back to Source.*"

"It's too hard. Why should I bother?"

"*You have forgotten the most important part of this story.*"

"Obviously."

"*It's tattooed on the palm of your hands in invisible purple ink.*"

"Not fair."

"*I know you.*"

"Yet, I sense you have just given me a slightly more advanced baby-in-the-tummy explanation of things."

"*Do you think the ancient Hebrews understood the formula $E = MC^2$?*"

"What about the more advanced cultures, like the Egyptians, Incans, or Mayans?"

"*A discussion for another time.*"

"I guess I don't have to understand cell division to believe that conception has taken place. After nine months, the proof arrives."

"*Proof of intelligent design is all around you, waiting to be revealed. Nature was the first Holy Book … layers upon layers of learning. The more you look, the more you will see that each day is filled with treasures—chance encounters, beach glass, even pain—as a way for you to open your eyes and remember …*"

"You've been trying to get my attention for a long time."

"*You are loved.*"

"Why is believing that so difficult?"

"If you want to evolve and receive the best goodies, you have to give up what the ego worships."

"Something about this feels familiar."

"You don't say …"

TEN

"Mm. Can you smell that?"

"Oz-God, you don't even have a nose."

"You do, though. What's your rush? We've been talking for hours."

"My tumor might explode any minute … then I'll never know the rest of the story."

"You're at the beach. Try to enjoy it."

"I don't smell anything. I think you're afraid that I can't handle what you're telling me."

"You've had quite a bit to deal with in the last twenty-four hours."

"So? Bring it on!"

"Close your eyes and take a deep breath."

"That scent you are pretending to smell is Mr. Zogs strawberry-scented surfboard wax—Sex Wax."

"Sex Wax?"

"Just a gimmick, but it gets your attention, right?"

"Sex on a surfboard sounds hazardous."

"Very funny. See that surfer?"

"The one with the yin and yang symbol tattooed on his deltoid?"

"Without wax on his board, he and his bimbo would slip off."

"Didn't you used to be one of those bimbos?"

"I was a brilliant bimbo."

"Oxymoron."

"How rude. I only used my bimbo-ness to lure handsome surfer boys into my lair."

"A bimbo by any other name ..."

"Aren't you being a bit judgmental?"

"Bimbo-ism is no different from intellectualism or any other -ism."

"OK, Mr. Heavy-pants."

"Guess I'm just too deep for you."

"Look at that guy now ... Wow."

"Try to rein in your lust."

"Why can't I ogle? I'm not hurting anyone ... Besides, I'm divorced."

"You ogled when you were married."

"I haven't looked this closely at a man in a long time. He looks so young and beautiful ... the graceful way he cuts in and out of the waves and his long, wet hair flying around his shoulders like velvet ropes. Yum."

"Go fantasize somewhere else."

"Jealous? You're probably old and white-bearded."

"No, that would be God the Father ..."

"Really?"

"No."

"Was Jesus good-looking?"

"You mean like the eye candy on the surfboard? No."

"You said *eye candy*. I might weep with joy."

"Intimacy based on eye candy is fleeting."

"At this moment, I believe you could exist."

"I know what makes you laugh. We are much closer than you think."

"What would I see if I looked at you?" I ask.

"I'm all the possible puzzle pieces. There are infinite aspects to my personality. I manifest in different ways for different purposes. You don't think Old Testament Yahweh would put up with your lip, do you?"

"So if you aren't God the Father ...?"

"Again, try to suppress your desire to put me into an intellectual box."

"You as *Father* doesn't work for me."

"There are lots of good men out there, Hope."

"I don't care about finding another man. Relationships are overrated. Soon that surfer-dude will grow a beer gut and go bald, and his wasp-waisted bimbo's boobs will sag and her skin will turn into wrinkled leather."

"A gloomy assessment."

"In my opinion, you have to enjoy the initial wave of lust in a relationship because after about six months, that fades, and the ugly truth emerges."

"And, of course, your behavior has nothing to do with creating this cycle of events?"

"Of course not."

"What are men to you besides sexy, abusive pigs?"

"Ouch. I guess I don't have much respect for the species."

"How's that panning out?"

"Ask Steve. Obviously, I screwed that pooch."

"Was your divorce really about his infidelity?"

"I guess not. As I said before, love has always been tangled up in a nightmare of sex and power."

"Do you like being a woman?"

"Hell no! Men are stronger—more respected. I hate to say it, but most women have to trade sex for a chance at love."

"Most women, or you personally?"

"I assume there are others like me."

"Your father did a terrible thing."

"I don't care. Why are you bringing him into this?"

"OK, what's your dream man like?"

"You should have seen Steve before we got married. He pursued me, listened to me, and bought me gifts for no reason. I had his undivided attention."

"He was your dream man?"

"He seemed so different from my father."

"There is much more to love than what you experienced as a child."

"OK, I've had enough of memory lane. I know I'm having a rough time with this divorce, but other than that, everything else is going pretty well. Besides, tolerable isn't so bad."

"If you say so."

"I am willing to concede that my story may warrant a deeper look—as long as you don't ask me to jump off the roof believing angels will catch me or some other crap like that."

"You do realize that almost every decision you make is based on faith. The raw oysters you ate yesterday could have given you hepatitis, yet you slurped them down. You aren't a stranger to faith, just faith in benevolent beings who have your best interest at heart."

"Why don't you guys do miracles anymore?"

"Sigh. Everybody wants a miracle. What's this conversation? Chopped liver? Sometime I'll show you how many times angels have swooped in and saved your butt."

"*Butt* sounds funny coming from you."

"If I'd known you would laugh this hard, I might have flashed my butt sooner."

"This helps."

"What?"

"You aren't slapping me around."

"Again, not my job."

"I have the freedom to practice any religion I want."

"Yes, you do."

"I'll admit to a Higher Power."

"Say what you're thinking."

"Gays have rights."

"Gay people have free will and deserve to be loved and protected, just like the rest of humanity."

"Exactly! The US Constitution protects our rights—at least it should."

"So, the Constitution is your Higher Power?"

"My brother, Ronny, is gay. He was attacked and almost killed by a truck full of high school kids."

"Hate is the antithesis of who I am. Free will can be unbelievably painful to watch."

"Cops should protect people from being assaulted."

"Isn't your father a policeman?"

"A woman has a right to choose what happens to her body."

"Are you making statements or asking questions?"

"I'm telling you what I believe."

"I know you're afraid."

"Stop implying that I can't handle things!"

"Why did you go to therapy?"

"I'm not finished discussing my rights."

"I know."

"I went because my marriage was falling apart, and Steve thought I had a drinking problem. I'm not afraid to admit it."

"So, you've faced those fears?"

"I stopped going when my therapist wanted me to talk about my childhood all the time. Believe me: I've already dealt with that."

"Had you been in therapy before?"

"Ages ago, way before Steve. I was depressed; stuff happened; you know how college is. One time I took some prescription pain pills after a party. My roommate found me in the bathroom. I must have dropped the bottle because there were pills all over the floor. Don't try and tell me angels knocked them out of my hand …"

"Remember your landlord at the time?"

"Oh, yeah, Butch or Bob something—a nice man. He helped get my drunken ass up the stairs a few times."

"Did you know that he prayed for you every day? Prayed for God to save your drunken ass?"

"What if he hadn't been praying for me?"

"Interesting question …"

"I don't want to know the answer."

"There are many people who would rather spend their entire lives defending a lie than admit they are powerless over something."

"I told you I'm not afraid to talk about my mistakes."

"Admitting powerlessness over your life is different from acknowledging your mistakes."

"Let's get back to my right to choose."

"Choose what?"

"Whether or not to get an abortion."

"Making love is a wonderful, freewill choice. However, it's complex. Three souls are involved. The consequences of conception can interfere with your life and cry and poop a lot."

"Obviously, but what if a woman is raped and she becomes pregnant, or what if a couple finds out their baby is horribly deformed? Isn't it better for the baby not to suffer?"

"Just for illustration's sake, let's say you know someone who has had an abortion."

"Yeah …"

"Why did this woman choose to terminate her pregnancy?"

"It was a mistake."

"The sex, the baby, or the abortion?"

"She didn't want to get married."

"Was she raped?"

"No. She was in college. Her whole life was ahead of her."

"Sounds scary."

"I thought it was the right thing to do at the time. Now I'm not so sure."

"If the baby had lived, how old would he be?"

"Ten, next month."

"Thank you for trusting me with your secret."

"There is nothing I can do to get my baby back. I feel like I've committed murder, even though 'they' say it isn't. I'll just have to live with it. What's done is done. A baby wasn't convenient. Oops, guess I'd better kill him off. I don't even believe in the death penalty, but I could do this?"

"Shh … stop now."

"No! I've done horrible things. I'm a drunk and a murderer! I had an affair with another professor and didn't tell Steve—just blamed him for everything. I don't deserve to live!"

"Come into the water with me."

"I can't. I'll drown."

"The choice is yours."

ELEVEN

March 3
Journal Entry

FEEL ANGRY AND REBELLIOUS. I MAY BE WISHY-WASHY ABOUT benevolent spirits, but I know for a fact that demons exist. I think dark beings are some of my oldest companions. Like judgmental relatives, all night they whispered in my dreams, reminding me of the shameful things I've done. OZ-God was right. I have plenty of faith … in evil and assholes.

Just before dawn, I went out to the balcony and screwed the top off a tiny liquor bottle and took a few sniffs before throwing it off the balcony into the pool. In case you've ever wondered, self-pity smells like scotch. In yet another fit of desperation, I scrounged around in my purse for the slip of paper with Rose and Slim's phone number on it.

Slim met me at the Island Café—bought me a shrimp omelet, and we shared a pot of coffee. He didn't make me talk much, thank God, just handed over his handkerchief when my sadness overflowed. I don't even know his last name; yet, because we share the same weakness, there is a bond.

He had to go to work a while ago, but now I don't feel so alone.

Walking out of the cafe, I see a hot-pink flyer imprisoned like a psychedelic butterfly under my windshield wiper. I leave it there, sitting in the car for a moment with the door open to let the heat bubble escape. Is this a message from heaven ... or some other place?

The writing on the flyer faces me—I read it through the glass and almost cough up my breakfast.

Guiding Light Tattoo and Crystal Emporium
Special Sale!
Buy two piercings — Get one free
We have books for your spiritual adventure!
Open noon to midnight

No turning back now. I'm fated to see connection points everywhere. After starting the car, I turn right on Tarpon Street and then left on Periwinkle before arriving at the Guiding Light. Wasn't there a soap opera by that name? This ought to be good.

The tattoo parlor is in a small, brightly painted clapboard house perched high on three-foot-tall cinderblock pylons. I zigzag up the warped and paint-chipped handicap ramp and open the door into hippie heaven.

A wave of patchouli, wind chimes, and Crosby, Stills, and Nash washes over me as I step across the threshold. On every table are different-sized clusters of quartz crystals and other multicolored minerals. Three walls of the room are covered with bookshelves and the other is papered with tattoo designs.

"Hi, I'm Dan."

The man slouching in the arched doorway is probably in his midsixties. He has wispy silver hair gathered into a thin ponytail tied with a piece of leather, and his amber eyes flash with interest, taking inventory of my completely unmarked arms, shoulders, and legs.

"Ah, a virgin ... unless you're hiding something."

"You have no idea," I say.

"Ready for some body art? Piercings are on sale."

"Yeah, I got the hot-pink memo."

The door tinkles behind me, and a beautiful Hispanic girl pours past me into the room.

"Just a sec," Dan says to me.

"Immaculata, are you ready for your final travail?" His face lights up as he hugs her.

She is young, barely out of her teens, and wearing a crimson halter top. She smiles as she walks past, and my breath catches when I see her back. From her neck down to the top edge of her low-rise jeans is an elaborate tattoo of the Virgin Mary draped in a cobalt-blue robe. Immaculata is not bony; roundness covers all the angles on her back, making it the perfect honey-colored canvas for such a portrait. She knows that I'm looking and stands very still, bowing her head as if in prayer.

"This is my greatest work. All we have left is the writing," Dan says.

"I've never seen anything like it." I say, not sure about correct tattoo etiquette.

"Hey, Dapper Dan, I can feel the Benadryl kicking in. Better get after it."

Immaculata yawns and stretches her arms up; the Virgin Mary tilts her head in an eerie way.

"Do you want me to go lie down?" she asks.

"Sure, I'll be there in a minute." Dan turns back to me. "Make yourself at home. There's some herbal tea over there. Look around. Take your time. You can watch me work on Imma if you want. She usually sleeps through the whole thing."

"Does it hurt?" I ask.

"Maybe the Virgin gives her strength." Straight white teeth appear from under his large mustache.

"Thanks. I'll just browse."

This is a supernatural setup—a cosmic production. I know it. The staging is perfect; the characters are rich, and the tattoo is perfect.

What role does my character play? Maybe I'm only a spectator. Should I get a tattoo? I will look for more clues.

I have read many of the books on the shelves—a New Age extravaganza of treasure maps I've already explored. Ah, Carlos

Castaneda, the beginning of everything for me. I thumb through one of the volumes. What was so profound? I remember … to find the Path with heart. When Don Juan and Carlos ate peyote buttons or smoked magic mushrooms, the physics of reality changed. I miss drugs …

Oh, *The Celestine Prophecy.* More of the same—reality is not as we perceive it; coincidences don't exist; we have access to so much more. This book focuses on looking for the connections between people and recognizing how things that seem random are actually tied together. Hm, kind of what Oz-God and I discussed on the beach? Next.

I can hear the low buzz of the tattoo machine. The music has changed to Joni Mitchell, her *Court and Spark* album. "My analyst told me—that I was right out of my head …" I sing along quietly.

"How are you doin' out there?" Dan speaks softly, but the house is small.

Sticking my head through the doorway, I smile. "Have you read all of your inventory?"

"Oh yeah, the classics. Are you a seeker?" Dan pauses, adding ink to the reservoir attached to the tattoo needle. I move closer to admire his handiwork and hear Immaculata's slow, heavy breathing. She must be asleep.

He points at Immaculata's back. "She has a long name."

"Who does?" I pause and then read aloud from the hem of the virgin's robe. "Santa Maria Immaculata."

"Yeah, but I don't think this young lady's a saint." Dan winks at me. There is no response from the tattoo virgin.

The buzz of the machine fills the room again, and I stand up to look at more designs taped to the wall. Celtic crosses, Catholic saints, Arabic, Hebrew, and Sanskrit words—Dan is an equal-opportunity artist.

"Have you been in my store before? You look familiar."

"Nope, never been here."

Dan looks at me over his half glasses and squints as if trying to read my aura. "If you say so."

"Maybe we knew each other in a past life," I blurt, turning away to hide my flaming face.

"You believe in reincarnation? Awesome ..." Dan nods his head a few times. I've obviously scored a point.

There is a groan from the table.

"Imma has a different philosophy from us ... tells me not to talk voodoo in front of her. By the way, what's your name?"

"Hope ... I know, cheesy."

"How long have you hated your name?"

"I don't know ... at least a couple of lifetimes." I laugh, flirting awkwardly. "I don't know that much about reincarnation—read a few books about Edgar Cayce when I was in college."

"Ah, the Sleeping Prophet. He was a Christian, you know." Dan says this directly to Immaculata's back.

"Probably a big hit at church," she mumbles from the table.

"In another time and place, I would have been burned at the stake for selling these books. God bless America, right?" Dan grins then leans his head from side to side, popping his neck.

For the first time, I notice his beautifully tattooed forearms—two sensuous jungles of shape and color winding up from his wrists and disappearing under rolled-up sleeves.

"What are *your* thoughts on reincarnation?" I ask Dan.

"I don't know ... It's kind of a comforting idea. None of us seem to be able to get it right the first time, and the idea that we can work stuff out over multiple lifetimes? I like that. It also provides one explanation for sudden or premature death."

"Yeah, but the idea of karma freaks me out a bit—every action, every thought, good or bad recorded in some great computer in the sky?" I shiver as if a ghost is walking through me. "Sounds like eternal judgment on steroids."

Dan continues with excitement. "No, you're missing the point! With reincarnation, there is no punishment—no judgment or finger wagging ... just more precious lifetimes to learn and balance it all."

"Maybe." I saunter around the room as if I don't care about any of it. "I guess if our souls were eternal, then, theoretically, we could look at the plus and minus karma columns and possibly participate in setting up or choosing our next lessons?" I raise my eyebrows, curious to hear his opinion.

He sits back on his stool—deep in thought while surveying his progress. "I really want to be a woman next time around."

"Why?" Immaculata and I say at the same time.

"To have babies, of course. Most women don't seem to appreciate how miraculous that is …"

My throat feels dry and tight.

"I do differ from what the Buddhists believe, however," he continues. "About reincarnation. I think that once you make it to a human body, you never go backward, like coming back as an ant or a pig or something."

"I had a past-life reading once," I say, half expecting lightning to hit the tattoo parlor.

"Who were you, Joan of Arc?"

"The one who heard voices in her head? No …" (I can almost hear Oz-God chuckling.)

"I wasn't anyone special, just a girl in Ireland in the 1300s."

"Do tell …" Dan bends back over his work.

"Evidently, I ran away from home because my parents wouldn't let me study with my brothers. I cut my hair, dressed like a boy, and walked to a monastery far away from my hometown."

"Radical, so did you get to study with the monks?"

"Oh yes, learned Latin and Greek—had a thing for plants and their medicinal uses, but one time a couple of the other monks saw me bathing in the river, and they were horrified—accused me of being a witch. One of my friends helped me escape," I say, feeling giddy.

"This is awesome, like a miniseries or something."

"I know, right? After that, I lived in the woods and became an herb woman—sort of a witchy midwife."

"Who performed your reading?"

"I studied for a summer with a group of metaphysicians on a farm in Missouri. It was intense. I learned a lot."

(Why am I showing off, telling this guy stuff I wouldn't admit to anyone?)

"You guys are so nuts." Immaculata bumps her forehead lightly on the table a few times. "I wish you could hear yourselves."

"Imma doesn't believe in anything but Jesus, do ya, honey?"

"Y'all just don't get it. He is the answer to all the questions."

I'm feeling feisty. "OK, I'll give you a shot, Immaculata. Enlighten us. Pretend I'm a Hindu who believes in reincarnation. How would you sell the Jesus idea to me?"

"Easy peasy."

"How old are you?" I ask.

Dan sighs deeply. "You're in for it, Hope. This girl has an answer for every question I've thrown at her."

"Out of the mouth of babes … Think you old fogeys can handle the truth?" she says, putting a fresh piece of gum in her mouth.

"Bring it on, young one." I smile at Dan and cross my arms.

"If I heard you bozos right, karma is like a huge list of all your sins—the good things and the bad things you've done, right?"

"Yes, in a simplistic sort of way," I say, and Dan nods.

"What do Hindus believe happens when they finally get it right—you know, after all the lifetimes of working things out?" Imma asks.

"Good question … Enlightenment? Hindu heaven?" Dan doesn't sound sure.

"It says here," I read from my phone, "that the goal of walking the karmic circle of light to dark and back again gives one a 360-degree understanding of love. Evidently, the only way to complete the cycle of birth and death is to understand life enough to have the compassion to love and forgive all things."

Dan looks at me with reverence.

I point to my phone. "Wikipedia … It's great."

"Would it be fair to say, then," Immaculata hops off the table and begins pacing, "that Hindus believe all humans are flawed from birth because of their karma?"

"Sounds about right." Dan stops Imma from pacing and applies a sterile covering over the new part of her tattoo.

"You must have been on the high school debate team," I say.

"UIL champion three years running! Now where was I?" She continues pacing.

"Original sin, or something similar," I add.

"Are you guys following, or do I need to slow down?" Imma hits Dan on the shoulder.

"You still haven't said what Jesus has to do with Hinduism." There is an edge in my voice. I can't help feeling a bit threatened by this Christian upstart.

"Obviously both of you are interested in the supernatural?" Imma makes a sweeping gesture toward the bookshelves.

Dan and I look at each other, nodding, and I add, "To a point, yeah."

"And you believe in a Supreme Being, God, a Higher Power? Then, is it too much of a stretch to contemplate that God, who created the world, could design a man who was born with a godlike ability to understand all things?"

"Are you referring to the Christian myth of Adam and Eve?" I say in a smug voice. (The ink isn't even dry on that conversation with Oz-God.)

Imma pulls her long hair into a sloppy bun on the back of her head. "Kind of. Jesus was like a second Adam, born with the ability to successfully understand the human condition without screwing everything up in the process."

"Do you mean, without creating karma?" I ask.

Imma nods and seems satisfied with her argument. I am not.

"OK, go on," I say.

"It's like he was evolved, you know, like from a higher plane of existence because he was part God." Immaculata seems frustrated by her lack of vocabulary. "It's all in the Bible—how to deal with life and our mistakes from an enlightened viewpoint."

"Aren't you being a bit simplistic? Besides, why would a Hindu believer be interested in—"

"I'll bet Mary Magdalene was quite an eye-opener for Jesus," Dan interrupts, smiling at me with soft eyes, and I remember that Immaculata is basically a high school girl.

Imma seems to be finished with us. "Don't be disgusting, Dan. Yes, Jesus was tempted—why do you think so much grace and mercy flooded Earth?"

"So why did God allow this perfect man, his *son* to be killed when he had so much to teach us?" I can't let this go.

"Karma, of course," she says flippantly, throwing our word back at us.

"But you said Jesus had no karma." I had her now …

"Not His karma. Ours—to show a way for *us* to be released from the past, present, and future karma of the whole world."

"That doesn't make sense either. If Jesus did that, then …" I feel pressure against my temples. All three of us seem to be enveloped in a mental whirlwind, and I can't stop my head from spinning.

Immaculate takes both of my jittery hands in hers. "If you choose to follow Him across the bridge He built, your sins are forgiven, cancelled right now, in this life, and when you die, you go to heaven or ascend or however you want to say it."

I can see that Immaculata believes what she is saying, but I feel as if I'm trying to breathe underwater.

"And that, ladies and gents, is why Jesus is the answer. Now, I have to go make churros." Immaculata counts out two twenty-dollar bills and kisses Dan's cheek. "Thanks for the tat, dude."

"I told you …" Dan's laughter is infectious.

"Churros?" I ask.

"Yeah, cinnamon fried donut thingies. Imma's mother owns a bakery."

Immaculata turns and stares at me from the front doorway. Her eyes are mature and inviting, strange for a teenager. "What's your name again?"

"Hope."

"Oh yeah. Don't worry. This God stuff is bigger than all of us. No way you're gonna get it all in one afternoon."

"Well, that's for damn sure," I mutter.

Imma pauses at the front door. "You know, Hope, you have the glow of something around you, but it isn't coming from your heart."

"Why not?" The news is strangely disturbing.

"Hey, Dan, this woman needs a tattoo. I'll pay."

"What? No, I'm kind of afraid of needles." I shudder.

"It doesn't hurt much … You definitely need a small heart with a cross in the middle, right here on the inside of your wrist." Imma places her fingers on her own pulse point. "Remember, love heals broken things."

"But …" Words fail me.

She waves at Dan. "I love you, old hippie. Quit wasting your life and come to Mass with Mama and me sometime."

The door tinkles. She is gone. Dan breaks open a package and takes out a new needle.

Now it's his turn to raises his eyebrows. "What color ink do you want?"

(Am I really going to do this?)

"Red … I guess."

"Cross too?"

"No, let's start with the heart."

TWELVE

THE MOON'S REFLECTION AT THE WATER'S EDGE PULLS AT MY womb where the day has settled, heavy and fertile. The tattoo didn't hurt as much as I thought it would. Afterward, Dan asked if I wanted to smoke some weed. I was tempted but felt that I was in an altered state already. Besides, it might trigger some binge drinking or something … That's what *they* say, anyway. Will I ever be free of *them?*

I must confess, back in the day, experimenting with drugs shifted something inside and connected me more to the earth and made me see the world in a new way. After smoking a joint, the simplest action or idea took on texture and meaning, becoming somehow sacred. For the first time, I was able to sense a universal force flowing through everything, not just people but rocks and plants and the ocean … everything.

I suspect, however, that with alcohol or any drug you're skipping steps and cutting in line, leaping unprotected into a seductive pit of razor-sharp mirrors that reflect a view of reality that tantalizes for a while but is only an illusion without action. Yep, always looking for a shortcut.

But if that's true, then why are mind-altering substances growing on our planet in the first place? Grapes, potatoes, grains, cedar berries, and even mold can be turned or fermented into wine and different liquors, not to mention marijuana, mushrooms, peyote, and opium poppies. Is mind alteration part of the Plan? A way to jump across dimensions? I wonder what Oz-God would say about that.

"Are you asking me a question?"

"Just ruminating. Why do psilocybin mushrooms grow out of cow patties?"

"Primo fertilizer, of course."

"Immaculata is something else."

"She reminds me of you."

"She should be the first woman Pope."

"Good idea."

"She's definitely on team Jesus, though ..."

"Your aura just constricted."

"The whole Jesus thing ..."

"Was it something he said?"

"No, it's all the woo-woo stuff surrounding Christianity, like a virgin conceiving and giving birth to an alien-type hybrid who rose from the dead and defeated the devil. Really? How could a disembodied spirit start a baby inside a human?"

"Just for the record, virgin has multiple meanings in ancient Hebrew."

"Besides a person who has never had sex?"

"It can also refer to a young, unmarried Jewish woman. Sexual experience isn't always mentioned."

"Why say that? Doesn't do much for your cause."

"My cause?"

"Spit it out. What is it you want to tell me?"

"How are babies made?"

"Back to this, are we?"

"I love quantum physics."

"Are we talking egg and sperm?"

"Sperm. Interesting little buggers."

"You're freaking me out."

"Be strong."

"Let's change the subject."

"Alien hybrid is a concept you are more comfortable with, yes?"

"Hey, one of my students told me that at one time angels were attracted to human females and did some interbreeding. It's in the Bible. Hey, technically, angels and their offspring are aliens."

"Yes, they are extraterrestrial in the true sense of the word. And godlike hybrids, called Nephilim were born from those unions."

"Bet that doesn't make it into many Sunday sermons."

"There is so much you don't remember yet."

"Remember?"

"In the dimension that I'm from, knowing and remembering are Siamese twins."

"Fundamentalist believers from all religions seem to pick and choose what suits their agenda. Just having something like Nephilim in the Bible makes me want to laugh at their pious posturing."

"As I said before, spiritual evolution is a process."

"To be fair, atheists aren't any better. I mean, come on. DNA is the end of the *random* debate. Something that elegant couldn't be from this world, much less a random combination of chemicals. I don't have to be religious to see that."

"Atheists, legalists, and proof-based scientists are operating solely on the three-dimensional Earth plane. I love them all so much, but there is so much more."

"But get with it, guys. Even I know that Earth isn't flat!"

"This is coming out of your mouth?"

"What? Yes I know there are 'flat-earthers' but round is just common sense."

"Finding compassion for the different levels and steps on every individual's spiritual journey might help balance your karma a little."

"So, you're a Hindu now?"

"You're a good boxer ..."

"Nope, not very athletic."

"You enjoy putting religious ideas, events, and huge classes of people into neatly labeled boxes."

"I think you have that backward. The religious ones have labeled me. They have cast *me* out and judged me as unworthy to be a part of their elitist group."

THIRTEEN

MY DAYS OF ESCAPING FROM THE REALITY BACK IN AUSTIN ARE numbered—this beach bubble will burst soon. In these past few days, my brain has expanded to include ... what? Tomorrow I check out of the hotel and return to what is left of my life. I let Steve stay in the haunted house we shared and have already moved into a two-bedroom apartment near campus. Who knew that my entire life could fit into fifty-five boxes?

When I leave, will Oz-God follow, or will my temporary insanity be over? All day I have avoided these questions but can't stop looking for the signs and wonders. I'm afraid that if I go any further into this fantasy, the things I love most about my life and identity will disappear—be absorbed into spiritual groupthink.

"You can run, but you can't hide."

"Oz-God, please don't act any weirder than you already are."

"Have you ever been on a scavenger hunt?"

"What do you mean? Like at a kid's birthday party?"

"Birthday party, spiritual quest—synonymous in your case."

"Now wait a minute! My quest has integrity. Scavenger hunt implies scrambling around sweating with a list of random items to hunt down."

"There is usually a prize."

"Yeah, a rubber whoopee cushion."

"How would you describe your journey so far?"

"Well, I obtained two college degrees in philosophy. I have studied many spiritual disciplines and expanded my understanding of the human mind ... OK, random scavenging does fit, I guess."

"There are no coincidences."

"Have you got a whoopee cushion for me in your big black bag?"

"You don't have to think of your choices as points on a predetermined line, remember? Each move forward is more like one dot inside a sphere of all possible choices—your next step could be on the outer edge or dead center."

"You must hang out with Deepak Chopra."

"We love that dude …"

"You keep saying *we*."

"Multidimensional implies more than one aspect."

"I'm assuming that the path at dead center is the closest choice to Truth?"

"Center has no meaning. All of the choices have consequences—some are better or quicker for your soul advancement than others."

"Finding the path with heart."

"Yes, Don Carlos."

"Do you know everything about me, even the books I've read?"

"Source God is Love, and love contains all. Do you get the concept of all? It includes everything about everything … forever."

"What if I choose to stay in one tiny corner of the sphere making bad choices?"

"We're sneaky. Besides, spheres don't have corners to hide in."

"I knew it."

"A portal to the spiritual world exists as an aspect of every choice—even the so-called bad ones. If you ever get tired of running away, you can find me in an instant."

"And if I refuse until I die?"

"If you choose to reject growth, the higher spiritual aspects of your DNA remain inactivated. The ego doesn't like to lose control and will always try to reinforce flesh over spirit. It can trap you across time."

"Sounds like hell to me."

FOURTEEN

"Who ya' talkin' to, lady?"

A small boy no taller than my waist stands a safe distance away, squinting at me in the afternoon sun.

"Hello, young man. What's your name?" I am glad to be chatting with a human being.

"That's personal, ma'am, but I'll give you my tank and cereal number."

"Do all those army men belong to you?"

"Yeah, my grandpa gave me about a hunnert of 'em. Wanna play army with me?"

I can't stop looking at this boy's sweet face. No child on earth could have eyes a more beautiful shade of blue. "Where are your parents?" Suddenly, I feel protective.

"Oh, they're out in the deep, dark water. I told them I'd stay here and guard the towels and stuff. Lots of eminies to look out for … Gotta bee-ware, ya' know?"

"Yes, I do—never know who you might run into on the beach."

The boy pauses as if considering for the first time that I might be one of those strangers his parents warned him not to talk to.

"Why are you alone?" he asks suspiciously. "Where's your kids?"

"I don't have any," I say, surprised by the twist of grief in my chest.

"Well, you gotta have a mommy. Where's she at?"

"My mommy's in heaven, but it's OK, I'm a grown-up."

The boy bites his bottom lip and nods, searching the sunset-kissed waves until he spots his parents.

"Sally, that's my dog, is in heaven. Maybe your mom can pet her sometime."

The boy's mother wades toward us, giving me a wary smile as she waves for him to come to her.

"Just a minute, Mom. Gotta get my men!" While his parents shake out their towels, the boy runs in every direction, scooping his soldiers into a yellow plastic bucket. I smile again and look away, feeling lonely. Will I ever find someone to be happy with? Maybe have children?

"Ma'am?" The boy has his chest puffing in and out, fists on his tiny hips. "Uh, it's gettin' dark soon. Might not be safe. Take this. He'll protect ya." He drops one of his army men into my hand and dashes off, making racecar sounds.

I look down at my green plastic protector, hysterical laughter rising in my throat. He has a rifle and is lying on his stomach like a sniper, ready to defend me from the tsunami-sized waves rolling toward us. I set the soldier on the sand and lie down on my stomach beside him, resting my upper body on my elbows like a sphinx. The wind whistles through my silver hoop earrings and blows my hair back.

An image of my mother superimposes itself over the view in front of me—Elizabeth Ann Franklin Delaney. She is young again and sitting on a picnic blanket. I don't think about her much since she died. We weren't close. She was a victim too. I confronted her once about not protecting me from my father … She claimed she never knew.

Is my mother in heaven, like the boy said? Is there a heaven? And what about hell? If the human soul is eternal, that would mean that insanity, despair, and loneliness don't end at death. Bummer. What would it be like to be tortured forever? What if all my cruel acts and moments of suicidal despair were dumped on me at my death, stripped of denial and rationalization and poured like battery acid on my soul?

Damp sand feels cold on my arms. The army man looks bigger up close. Whoever designed this toy put a lot of detail into his facial expression—he looks a little panicky, like he knows he's going to die but will go down defending what he believes. I'm jealous. I'm still not sure what I believe.

What about my quest? Am I a scavenger without a cause? Did I get to the threshold of enlightenment and trip? This can't be right. Every cell in my body screams for more. It feels like dying. What if this is my last chance?

Me, me, me. The seagulls mock. I can see three of them picking at a fish carcass. What if activating the God particle of my DNA *is* evolution—survival of the fittest? If we as a species ignore it … we die out, we become extinct, and our empty souls are left to rot on Earth with Satan and the rest of his fallen angels. I have no idea what parts of the ancient paradigm to hang onto.

FIFTEEN

MY HOTEL ROOM IS DARK AND FEELS CLAUSTROPHOBIC. FROM my window I see a few oil rig lights on the horizon blinking slowly—a steady SOS across the dark water. My future beckons.

How will this experience translate when I jump back into the Mixmaster of my life? Where is the instruction manual for those of us who insist on coloring outside of the lines? Maybe it's true that everything—people, books, and belief systems—reflects pieces of the puzzle.

There must be a Bible in one of these drawers ... I don't have to be afraid that opening it will suck my will to live and make me a God-zombie. From now on, I commit to renewing my quest for Truth and approach all religions like an anthropologist looking for the missing links.

Suddenly, someone pounds on my hotel room door with both fists, and I drop the Bible and scramble to open it.

"Please, come now!" The teenage girl can hardly speak. Her face is completely drained of blood.

"What is it?" I say, running barefooted behind her and through the open door next to mine.

"It's Bobby. He must have fallen in the tub ... I don't know ... I was on the balcony."

I almost slip in the hallway. Bobby is lying naked on the bathroom floor. Along the edge of the tub are green plastic army men.

The girl begins to hyperventilate. "I'm just the babysitter; I work for the hotel. I tried to call the front desk, but all the lines are busy."

"Use your cell phone and call 911 now!"

Bobby's face is turning blue. He isn't breathing. Oh, dear God, no!

"Bobby, can you hear me?" I try to recall my boring CPR classes. The skin on the side of his neck is ice cold, but there is still a pulse.

"God, help me. Don't let this boy die!" I compress his chest—one, two, three, four, five—and then pinch his nostrils shut and breathe air into his small lungs.

"This boy believes in you, damn it!" One, two, three, four, five, breathe. "Get me a blanket!" I yell at the babysitter.

Bobby's head jerks and water sprays out of his mouth onto my face and chest. He takes a breath, coughs, and gasps again.

"It's all right, sweetheart. You're fine now." I take the blanket from the girl's shaking hand and wrap it around him. He shivers and hides his face in my wet shirt, crying.

"I w-w-was playing … s-s-s-standing up in the tub. D-D-Daddy's gonna be mad."

"Nobody's mad. Shh, now." I hear the squawk of paramedics on their walkie-talkies coming down the hall. The babysitter is crying. I rock Bobby back and forth.

"Hey, you're that lady from the beach." His eyes light up for a moment.

Two EMS men gently take him from my arms and carry him into the other room.

"Are you the boy's mother?" one of them asks.

I put my back against the wall and hug my knees while tears stream down my face. "No, I'm next door."

"Do you know the parents' names?"

I point vaguely. "The babysitter …"

The man leaves the bathroom, and I hear the girl giving them the parent's information.

"Their name is Diamante, D-I-A …"

"We've got it, Diamante."

"They left a cell phone number somewhere, but I couldn't find it. I was only out on the balcony for a minute, talking to my boyfriend. If my battery hadn't been low ..."

I hear the girl start crying again. Poor thing. The what-ifs will haunt her forever.

I slowly get up and walk into the living room. Bobby is lying on the couch where a black-clothed man takes his vital signs and checks a good-sized bump on his head. Bobby looks terrified. Seeing his pajamas on the dresser, I walk over to the man who is now writing on his clipboard.

"Here are Bobby's PJs."

"We need to take him to the hospital as soon as possible."

"Can I dress him first?"

"If you hurry. By the way, good work in there." He flashes me a smile without really looking at me. "It's hard to find people these days who can think on their feet."

"I didn't save him." I can barely hear my own dazed voice. "Something ... Someone else saved him."

The paramedic is silent. His pen stops moving and he looks at me, probably wondering if I'm in shock. I let him take my pulse and shine his penlight in my eyes before going back to his paperwork.

"So, Bobby, you like Spiderman?" I try to sound normal as I scoot next to him on the couch. His arms are so small and thin, I'm afraid they will break as I help him find the armholes in his pajamas. He is still clutching one of his army men. This one is standing up and looking through binoculars. Bobby isn't blue anymore but still shivers.

"Diamante, is that your last name?" I ask

"Do you know where Mom and Dad are?"

"They're almost here."

"Diamante means diamond in I-talian," he says, teeth chattering.

I smile. Bobby cocks his head as if remembering something and crooks his finger at me to come closer. I lean in so he can whisper his sweet living breath in my ear.

"Jesus tole me something when I was in that sunshiny place."

"What did he say?" Now I'm shivering.

"He said, 'Tell the pretty lady from the beach that Oz–God says hello.'"

DIAMOND DUST

SIXTEEN

June 10
Journal Entry

CONFESSING TO THE CRIME WAS AGONY. TALK ABOUT SUFFERING the consequence of a horrific choice … "We're going to let you go," the philosophy chairman told me, "and give you some time to get back on track."

Oh, thanks, assholes. I'd rather fight my way through a pit of vipers than face those colleagues again. I was trying so hard to stay sober, to rebuild my life, and then, well, shit … I'll try to describe it before my sugarcoating ego rationalizes the truth.

Thankfully, most of what happened that night is obscured by an alcoholic blackout. I came back from the beach with some good months of sobriety behind me, so it is a terrifying mystery as to how I ended up at the spring faculty party with a beer in my hand. A bottle of stolen bourbon later, every shred of my newfound sanity went … Poof!

I remember a rooftop somewhere, maybe on campus. I could see the sparkling stars swirling and then … a flash, and I was trying to escape from a cop with a gun. If he hadn't grabbed me, I might have fallen off the roof.

I woke up on the floor in a nasty jail cell with the reek of sour beer, blood, and vomit coming from my hair. The gritty concrete messed up my face, and my jaw felt cattywampus, making it hard to talk or even sip a blessed drop of water.

Colorful taunts from my cellmates reminded me of things I'd said the night before—evidently there were insults, shoving, and, finally, some other drunk chicks beat me up.

"But why?" one might ask. What about cleaning up my act and all the other woo-woo crap?

Who the hell knows? Despite all my education, nothing positive seems to stick. Am I constitutionally incapable of healing? I thought that I'd stumbled onto some answers. I was waaay wrong …

SEVENTEEN

NIGHTTIME IN THE DESERT OF SOUTH TEXAS IS UNNERVING AS it enfolds me in its dark cloak, drawing me away from my journal and out onto the tiny front porch. I tentatively move down the steps—my paranoid bat ears alert to any sound of menace. In the few weeks since school ended and I was banished into purgatory for the summer, I've felt perpetually hungover—even though I've been without alcohol, *again,* for twenty-one days.

A black rhinoceros beetle the size of a baby shoe twists and wiggles on its back in the gray dust beneath a buzzing mercury vapor light near my temporary dwelling. I had no idea that insects could grow to such nightmarish proportions. With hairy bug legs in the air, it tries to flip over. I know just how it feels.

"You could die out here …" I hear a man growl from behind an abandoned chicken coop.

Fred Masters, the craggy, bowlegged cowboy from the World's End Ranch who drove me from the bus station to my summer job, grabs my arm.

"Son of a—don't *do* that!" I yell, almost dropping my flashlight.

I like Fred. He's an old-school flirt, and we've already built a shaky rapport. I doubt that he knows about my recent arrest; then again, maybe that's why he likes me.

Fred cackles and, with precision, spits brown tobacco juice on the ground near my flip-flops.

"Nice, Fred. Thanks."

"Just aimin' to please. What are you cattin' around in the dark for, anyhow?"

"I could ask you the same thing, old man."

"Junior and Manny want me to check on the mares tonight. Two of 'em are 'bout to foal."

Fred tosses his head toward the barn behind the ranch foreman's house. Yellow light glows from the hayloft, and I can just make out the backlit shadow of someone leaning against the windowsill.

"Who are they?" I ask.

"Look at you ... been here a week and don't know shit from Shinola."

"What are you talking about?"

"Never you mind, Missy. Manuel is solid but best steer clear of Junior. He's too much for you to handle."

"Yeah, right ... whatever." With a toss of my hair, I turn and catch my flip-flop on a rock and stumble. Dammit ... how cliché.

Smirking, Fred shakes his head and hobbles toward the barn.

I am grateful for the darkness ... and my flashlight. The problem is that I *am* afraid of all the things that go bump in the night, especially since my powerlessness wears so many disguises. Half-dead memories still scratch at the door of my soul: their cracked and childish voices whisper, "Mustn't speak! Don't tell!"

Safely back on my front porch, I collapse in a wicker rocker. For a moment, the whirring fan overhead twists me away from my distress. Why didn't I just jump off that philosophy building? Pitiful follow-through. After taking one step forward, now I'm fifty miles back. I thought Oz-God was going to save me ... "Red rover, red rover, let Hope come over!"

"Sure, I'll play!" Then reality shows up, slamming me back into the wicked strongholds of my past. My bones ache with anxiety and the humiliating proof that I can't be fixed. I'll settle for a summer's worth of peace ... Besides, no one down here knows my story.

"How many nightmares are you going to sweat through before we talk about what happened?"

"Oh, hi, Oz–God ..."

"Hi, yourself."

"I can't believe you showed up. You have every right to be mad at me."

"I believe you're the angry one."

"I messed up."

"You were lucky. Drunk and disorderly is only a class III misdemeanor. They could have added resisting arrest."

"But that policeman grabbed me! I don't know why I drank that first beer."

"The alcoholic's conundrum ..."

"I tried to be good. I went to meetings even when I didn't want to."

"Rough alcoholics at those meetings?"

"It was an AA meeting for professionals, doctors, lawyers, and even some of the professors from work. I couldn't be myself."

"A meeting of professional alcoholics ... hmmm. No wonder."

"You're *so* witty!"

"Your ego will fight to the death."

"I'm tired. My mental fingers are bloody from compulsively feeling for the sharp edges of things I've done or left undone."

"OK, hand over the switchblade."

"What?"

"No more stabbing yourself."

"I can't stop."

"I know everything you've done and still love you."

"Yeah, but you're different."

"I don't count?"

"Sort of ... I don't know why other people's opinions matter so much."

"Try to imagine me putting my celestial hand over your flapping lips for a moment, OK?"

"Sorry."

"Why did you stop interacting with me? Suddenly, you were hiding ... I was seeking, and all I heard were crickets."

"I knew you wouldn't want me until I cleaned up."

"How's that misconception working for you?"

"My chest feels wet and fluey inside—like unspeakable things are growing there."

"Be still."

"The other day, an old drinking buddy asked, 'Do you think you're better than us now?' She seemed afraid that I might try to infect her with something."

"You know how it feels to be afraid of change. Is that the reason you got drunk?"

"Not consciously."

"And now?"

"I'm done with all this."

"All what?"

"You, this merciless digging ..."

"Don't count on it."

EIGHTEEN

THOUSANDS OF EMPTY ACRES PRESS IN, SURROUNDING ME WITH nature's version of dry humor. Not sure the joke is funny. Lumpy white clouds sit on the horizon like Sunday morning slackers—disinterested, while parched mesquite trees strain upward, clawing for moisture with their thorny fingers. I must admit that being in the desert is a welcome change of pace … stimulating my creativity.

What do I text to friends back in Austin about my unexplained absence? Oh wait, do I still *have* any friends? *Pseudosabbatical* has a nice ring to it and is a noble and privileged thing in academia. I'm taking some time off to rest and increase my wisdom. Yeah, that's the ticket.

"Denial is not a river in Egypt."

"OK, Oz-God, fine. I thought I was boarding the love train with you, not thumbing a ride on the hay wagon to hell."

"How long have you been working on that sentence?"

"Shut up."

"How's the writing coming?"

"Look, there's a chicken!"

"That good, eh?"

"No one wants to hear about a woman who got a second chance at life and then immediately jumped off the cliff into more criminal behavior. Do you know how hard it is to be banished back to square one?"

"Failure is often built into foreword movement."

"What's that supposed to mean?"

"Remember kindergarten? Often you had to do it wrong to learn how to do it right."

"That's not very encouraging. I'm a mature woman."

"Humiliation can be a powerful motivator."

"You could have warned me."

"Yeah, I could've said, 'Hey, Hope, I checked the crystal ball today, and the odds are you're going to go home and blow it!'"

"You're right. I wouldn't have responded well."

"Your ego is still in charge … wielding its free will to get drunk and ignore your inner voices."

"And now I'm screwed."

"Bet you didn't know that self-pity is the flip side of arrogance."

"Don't you ever stop?"

"Hey, enjoy! You're on sabbatical!"

"This environment is so different from the ocean, so dry and empty."

"My cathedral is the vast vault of blue overhead."

"Show-off. You've got the whole world in your hands. What do I have?"

"Hope, the misery mass has ended. Go in peace."

"Funny."

"The choice to drink will always be there."

"Alcohol is a war I can't win."

"I'm sure the university police are relieved to hear you say it."

"Don't rub it in."

"I don't have to. You've been picking that scab for weeks."

"Isn't forty days in the desert supposed to be time of spiritual awakening? This feels like punishment."

"Do you realize how close we are to the border of Mexico?"

"Should I be afraid?"

"Can you say powerless and unmanageable in Spanish?"

"My brain hurts, and my vision is blurry."

"Admit it. You upset that I didn't wave my wizard wand."

"Maybe. So?"

"Now you have a new excuse to blame the effects of your bad choices on punishment from God. Free will for Earthlings? What were we thinking?"

"I'm just as neurotic sober as I was drunk. It pisses me off."

"Didn't you have rosy hopes and dreams? Remind me what those were again."

"Don't change the subject. Besides, what's wrong with slamming the lid on the past? It's over, I survived, move on ... But I can't because you've wedged your big fat foot in the door."

"My fat foot loves you."

"Go away."

"Really?"

"No, just kidding. Maybe not kidding."

"As long as you're clear about the matter. I wonder what your chronic headaches are about?"

"Why can't a headache just be a headache?"

"Your body is the parakeet in a coal mine. Warning! Warning! It's kind of awesome."

"Please, no more metaphors."

"Look, you've come to a roadblock. Brain sirens are screaming to get your attention."

"You are saying that every ache and pain is my fault? Figures ..."

"You don't see, yet, how intricately your mind, body, and spirit are connected."

"So, people with cancer have brought disease upon themselves?"

"It's impossible not to participate in some aspect of disease. Even ignoring your issues can compromise the immune system and cause self-destruction at a mental, physical, or spiritual level."

"Now those are some hot-button topics, although I *can* see that cancer is an indicator of imbalance ..."

"Learning to understand your own body language can become a life-or-death issue."

"It's much easier to blame someone like you or my abusive childhood."

"If you hit your thumb with a hammer, it will hurt every time."

"What? Your illustrations make me crazy."

"To hope and pray that the next time you get smashed by one of your choices, one of us will swoop down and change the laws of physics so that it doesn't hurt? Magical thinking."

"Fine. I get it."

"I am able to do magic in your terms. Someday you will too. But in the case of your most recent arrest ..."

"My only arrest, thank you. DUIs don't count."

"Do you think you might have had a part, consciously or unconsciously, in setting up a learning experience?"

"I plead the fifth."

"Put down the hammer ... at least for this desert sojourn."

"I can't decide which is worse—my past or skipping into this present pile of excrement."

"Skipping? Has there been some skipping? Must have turned my head for thirty-something years and missed it."

"You're *such* a crack-up."

"Hate to be the scary clown at kindergarten graduation, but no one escapes life's lesson."

"Trapped like rats."

"At least I know the way out of the maze."

"Oh yes, treasures and tasty food pellets abound."

"Holding onto secrets can be exhausting, don't you think?"

"Back off. I've already given my sponsor a personal inventory of my past. All the pain should be gone. Instead, I've found a new killing field with bones buried everywhere."

"There is nothing new about what's buried inside you."

NINETEEN

ULA AND MICAH FLANNIGAN ARE THE RANCH OWNER'S children. Seven and ten years old, their shiny yellow hair and clover-colored eyes make me think of two Lucky Charms—magically delicious. Their homeschool education has become my part-time summer job.

"You won't find any arrowheads." Micah talks over his shoulder at me, strutting ahead as we set out on the path to an Indian burial ground. Slung bandolier-style across his back is the new BB gun his father bought him over the weekend.

"Why not?" I ask.

Dula puts her small hand in mine, tugging until I lean down. "Because you're so serious," she whispers.

I laugh. "Well, seems to me arrowhead hunting is pretty serious business, right?"

Dula sighs and purses rosy lips, swinging her blonde pigtails back and forth across her cheeks. "You'll see." She squats and picks up a perfect bird point that I have walked right past and hands it to me. "Here. This one might bring you luck."

The sky is clear, and the afternoon sun sears all exposed skin. Bring it on. I pull the sleeves of my T-shirt up on my shoulders to avoid a farmer's tan.

Dula picks up another arrowhead made from a deep red stone. All the rocks and flint chips at my feet blend; maybe she sees them better because she's closer to the ground.

"Dula, honey, how do you do that?"

She smiles, and subtle light flashes across her face. "It's easy."

"Not for me. We've been out here for thirty minutes, and I haven't even found a broken one."

"I *told* you!" Micah yells from somewhere in the brush up ahead.

"If I tell, you can't laugh." Dula looks toward the bushes where her brother's disembodied voice came from.

"Is it funny?"

"I can *hear* them," she says.

"The arrowheads? Really?"

"Uh-huh … they sing to me."

Suddenly, I feel like dying from her cuteness—literally melt into a lump.

"Can you hear any singing right now?"

Dula lifts her perfectly shaped chin and closes her eyes, letting her hands hang at her sides. A breeze blows some stray hairs across her face. She turns abruptly and starts walking.

"Are they over there?" I ask.

"*Shh!* The wind is telling me which way to go."

Who is this holy being dressed as a little girl? Why can't I hear the arrowheads sing? Oh yeah, because I'm full of shit.

We come to a small rise. Dula sits on a flat rock and pulls a small apple from the pocket of her overalls.

"Aren't you going to look for more?" I am excited, expecting to see diamonds glittering at her feet.

"No, I'm hungry. You go ahead." To take a bite out of her apple, she must gnaw with one side of her mouth because her front teeth are missing.

"I like the broken arrowheads now," Dula says as she wipes apple juice off her mouth with the back of her hand. "Mama taught me how to make pretty things with them … before she went to heaven."

"Hey, guys, lookee here!" Micah is leaning over an ant bed alive with frantic activity.

Dula ambles over and squats to see better.

"Don't get too close—they might bite you," I warn.

Micah unhitches his BB gun and aims at the colony.

"No, sir, Micah. We aren't murdering our hard-working fellow creatures today. Come on. Let's follow this ant trail and see where they're going."

Dula lags behind me. "I don't see why they call it an ant bed. They look too busy to be sleeping." Her eyebrows scrunch together. She has her father's full bottom lip.

My throat feels tight again.

"Gah, Dula, you're so stupid!" Micah throws a rock nonchalantly, as if he isn't aiming for the anthill.

"*Stupid* is a dirty word. I'm gonna tell Daddy."

I feel uneasy about reprimanding either of them, so I redirect their attention. "Look, they're still traveling way up here."

"Those guys are probably a hundred ant miles from their base," Micah says.

"Ooh! There are itty-bitty ants over here. Are they the babies?"

Micah rolls his eyes and starts to say something to his sister, but I raise my eyebrow at him, and he shuts his mouth.

Dula continues, "Miss Hope? Do big ants eat little ants?"

"I don't know. We'll have to look it up when we get back to the house."

Micah turns around, walking slowly back to the original anthill. "This one has a seed or something in his mouth," he says. "It's gonna take him all day to get home. What a waste of time."

"Not a waste at all," I respond.

Should I teach these children a bit of truth? I take a deep breath.

"Micah, don't you know what will happen when that ant makes it back to his colony? He'll be a hero. The other ants will probably let him take his treasure directly to the queen for her dinner."

"Yeah!" Dula parrots me. "He'll be a hero." She turns back to stick her tongue out at her brother and instead screams and drops her apple.

Micah is standing over the anthill—peeing on it.

"Who's the hero *now?*" He laughs.

TWENTY

CRUISING THE WORLD WIDE WEB THIS MORNING, ON THE WAY to "do big ants eat little ants," I googled *adobe*, which is basically a house made of mud and straw, baked by the sun into bricks. Oz-God better protect this little piggy before some other interdimensional monster starts huffing and puffing to blow me down.

Through the window of my mud hut, I have a pristine view of the western sky. I really don't mind that I'm on the far edge of nowhere, where the coyotes howl and the rattlesnakes slither. Just kidding. I'm petrified. I don't know how big this ranch is, and Micah told me it's rude to ask.

Today, a memory sits in the blind spot to the left of my mind's eye. Analyze? Fail. My thoughts are attention-deficit preschoolers at recess. Hm, preschoolers are children—I may know what I'm avoiding ... just don't know if I have the energy to clean up that specific mess.

"Blind spot?"

"Don't you ever sleep, Oz-God?"

"I might miss something."

"Why can't I download a black hole icon and drag and drop my character defects?"

"Bad memories can be deleted from your active files, but unless you transmute them—"

"They bubble up from the hard drive like satanic black goo."

"*Such wonderfully graphic images … Has anyone ever encouraged you to write?*"

"Nice try."

"*Hope springs eternal.*"

"Why don't you just tell me what to do?"

"*Lazy butt.*"

"How do I get *over* this crap?"

"*You can start by calling your demons by name.*"

"Like pets?"

"*Or peeves …*"

"Let's see. Dopey, Grumpy, Sleazy, Murderer … Shall I continue?"

"*Hidden under the sarcasm are lost pieces of yourself.*"

"I know … more of the fat and disgusting puzzle pieces."

"*Only disgusting if you look through offal-colored glasses.*"

"Fine, I'll admit that there may be more shitty memories in here."

"*It's a process.*"

"When will it be enough for you?"

"*This isn't about me.*"

"My head just burst into flames."

"*I saw the beautiful cross you and Dula made yesterday. Tell me about that.*"

"I don't understand how those kids can be so amazing. At least I had a mother."

"*No one escapes the lessons, remember?*"

"But they're so young."

"*So were you.*"

"Anyway, Fred took us to the scrap pile, and we picked out some pieces of wood so Dula could make a cross to decorate her mother's grave. She encouraged me to make one too."

"*Pretty crafty, that little one.*"

"First we painted the wood with bright colors and then glued fake jewels, beads, and broken arrowheads all over them."

"*Was it fun?*"

"Oh man, love that bling … but then Dula asked me who my cross was for, and I started to cry. The only image in my head was my unborn baby. She asked me why I was sad, and I told her my child had died. But it wasn't a child. It wasn't anything when I—"

"Then what did Dula do?"

"She crawled up in my lap and cried with me. I can't describe how painful and precious it was. I never want to go through that again!"

"Which part?"

"I didn't think of my abortion as murder at the time. I guess I had to rationalize those feelings so I could survive."

"You just named one of your demons."

"Abortion is a demon?"

"It is to you. Sharing your grief with Dula—your losses—puts you both on the road to healing."

"I do feel better."

"That's the alchemy of compassion."

TWENTY-ONE

"WELL, LOOK WHAT THE CAT DRAGGED IN," FRED SAYS with one of his ancient, dust-covered boots cocked up on the side of a concrete water trough. The wire brush in his hand drips with strings of green algae.

"What's with it with you and cats, Fred?" I ask, pleased that I remembered to wear tennis shoes today.

"Well, you know what they say … Beware of men who hate cats."

"Why should I worry about that?"

"You figure it out." Fred spits. "I s'pose it'll be me that has to drive you and the kids to the hoedown tonight."

"The what? No one mentioned any hoedown to me. Besides, I'm sure I don't have the right outfit."

"Who cares what you wear? It's gonna be a wing dinger."

I start walking away from Fred. I don't want to go to a party! There will be drinking and men … and I'll have to make small talk and be charming. I'll tell Mr. Flannigan that I feel sick or can't be around alcohol … No, that would remind him I'm an alcoholic and …

"Look! Turkey vultures have decorated that cell tower! Looks like poo-flocking on a Tim Burton Christmas tree."

"Thanks, Oz-God. Your attempts at diversion are as bad as mine. Besides, what do you know about Tim Burton?"

"Did you really just ask me that?"

"Speaking of creepy, last night I dreamed that I died. Do you want to hear about it?"

"Were there circus performers?"

"Uh, no … but it *was* scary."

"No elephants in the room?"

"What is your deal today? Anyway, in the dream this black-robed character was gathering Steve's dismembered body parts, my shredded credit cards, diplomas, and broken trophies and stuffing everything into a black body bag. The ghoul zipped it up and dragged it to the curb."

"Bring out your dead!"

"I'm not dead yet."

"Are you sure?"

"I do feel the skin on my face peeling back."

"Peek-a-boo."

"Thanks for showing up at my pity party."

"Maybe you should spend a couple of months doing some focused and intense wallowing."

"Would you give me a medal at the end?"

"And extra stars for effort."

"I can't help it if there's a piñata of problems hanging in my closet. All I seem to do is pace back and forth in front of the locked door with a baseball bat."

"Your perceived badness is in there."

"It's a bloody mess."

"Then why do you keep fondling the key instead of letting the monsters out?"

"Why do I have to exhume the bodies?"

"Nobody wants to open their smelly can of whoop-ass."

"You could give me a get-out-of-the-closet-free card."

"I have."

"Maybe I'm addicted to angst."

"What is your self-pity really about?"

"I feel depressed because of what keeps happening to me. Why shouldn't I feel sorry for myself? No one else protected me, stroked my hair, and told me everything would be OK."

"*Self-pity can be its own reward ... until you replace it with something better.*"

"Why am I connected with you but still in pain? I see other people, religious and otherwise, who bitch and moan and then win the lottery. Why not me? This feels like a curse. I want to quit all this spiritual mess, but you've kind of ruined me ... Hey, are you listening?"

"*Don't mind me—I'm over here watching this dung beetle play with his poop.*"

"That's just rude."

"*I didn't want to interrupt.*"

"You talk about poop a lot."

"*Must be something in the air ...*"

"Maybe I do need a diversion."

"*No comment.*"

"Sometimes an unexamined life is good, right?"

"*Wrong. Nada. No.*"

"I can't see clearly right now anyway. Tonight, I'll be a pirate on the open sea ... 'Arggh! It's into the blind spot with ye!'"

"*Uh ...*"

"The beach seems like so long ago."

"*We've had a slam-bang start.*"

"I haven't changed very much."

"*Are you kidding?*"

"Really?"

"*All the cool people spend time in the desert.*"

"The desert is lonely ... Feels haunted."

"*Hm. Could that be the point?*"

"I'm traveling toward the heart of darkness."

"*Git! Go to the barbeque already!*"

TWENTY-TWO

"**M**ISS HOPE, WHAT ARE THOSE MEN DOIN'?"
Dula has dressed up in a short, blue jean skirt with a red-and-white-checkered ruffle sewn onto the hem. She scuffs her red cowboy boots in the dust—a sure sign that she is nervous.

"They are throwing horseshoes at those metal stakes stuck in the ground, see?"

I don't have any boots to shuffle. This really *is* my first rodeo.

Dula thrusts out one of her tiny hips and chews on the tip of her pigtail. "Why did they steal the horse's shoes?"

Just then, Micah swaggers up to the pitching line and a couple of grown men chuckle and elbow each other.

"Ready to play with the big boys, Micah?" one of them asks.

Micah spits and holds the horseshoe up to his face. Closing one eye, he takes aim and lets it fly. It clanks against the stake before spinning on one of its ears and landing a couple of inches away. "God-dawg it!" he says turning red.

"Still a whippersnapper!" one of the men teases.

"I'd like to see you do better," Micah mumbles.

I sense the man behind me before he whooshes by, striding directly toward Micah. There is something vaguely familiar about him. He smells like good cologne, a campfire, and maybe a few drops of diesel gasoline. I should write romance novels.

The man places his hands on the boy's shoulders and says something in a quiet voice to the group. I can't see his face, only the rear view of a typical movie star cowboy—broad shoulders, dark hair, and well-fitting Levi's. The men laugh, and Micah's body relaxes. Dear Lord, can I have a cowboy like that in my Christmas stocking? Before I can ask Dula who he is, she runs off toward the food and music.

The party feels like a statewide event. Who are all these people, and where did they come from? It's hard to imagine that one hundred miles of emptiness have produced such a crowd, although the ranch does have an airstrip; we passed it on the way in. I keep expecting to see a former president or at least a congressman at the guacamole table.

People are dancing or standing in groups. Women playfully poke their partners in the chests or slap at their beefy arms—pretending to be offended by something they have said. Ancient mating rituals.

There are two buffet lines and probably thirty-five tables with colorful paper flowers in hand-glazed Talavera pots at the center of each. Super-sized napkins match the red, blue, and green tablecloths, and dozens of people are sitting in white wooden folding chairs drinking, laughing, and wiping barbeque sauce off their faces. Did Norman Rockwell ever paint Texas?

From two separate open bars, the mixed scent of Carta Blanca beer and good bourbon wraps itself around my neck like a silk scarf. Men, dancing, and alcohol are not a good mixture for me. Why can't I have just one? Oh yeah …

I must escape this merriment. While ignoring a few curious stares, I force my hands into busyness by stacking empty plates. Now, where is the kitchen?

As I teeter with my tower of dishes up the back entrance of the sprawling ranch house, a five-foot-tall ball of fire waving a wooden spoon almost runs over me while chasing two men in cowboy hats out of the door. The spoon smacks one of the men's shoulders and cracks in half.

"Otto, look what you made me do!" The woman tries to glare but has to bite her lip to keep from cracking up.

Stunned, I watch the men shrug and lumber off, waving and laughing as the woman bends down and picks up the pieces of her spoon.

"This was my favorite spoon! I used to spank my baby girl's bottom with this spoon." The woman looks off into the distance as if her child were, at this moment, riding off into the sunset. She finally notices me standing with my plates.

"Good Lord, I'm sorry! Thank you so much, although it wasn't necessary. We have a tribe of people on the clean-up committee."

The short woman is probably in her sixties, but with her smooth and well-taken-care-of skin, she looks much younger, especially for someone who works in a hot kitchen. Her shoulder-length silver-blonde hair is twisted into a loose knot on top of her head, and a few strands have fallen around her face. Impossibly thin arms disappear into elbow-high oven mitts.

Opening one of the stainless steel ovens, she lifts a huge foil covered pan of tamales out of its fiery depths.

"Here, let me help you!" I stash the plates in one of the sinks and rush around the king-sized chopping block in the center of the kitchen, but she has already set the pan on waiting hot pads.

"You shouldn't be lifting those heavy pans. Where is the rest of the catering crew?" I ask.

"Partying with the guests, I assume." She smiles and wipes her small hand on a large apron before extending it toward me. "You're a godsend. My name is Nell. Who are you?"

Clear gray eyes lock with mine. There are no furtive glances at my ragged, unpainted fingernails or lack of appropriate hoedown attire. Her quick handshake is firm.

"I'm Hope."

"Just when I think I'm doomed!" Her laugh is real and has a surprisingly dainty snort at the end.

"Isn't God funny?" she says, shaking her head as she hands me an apron.

"A riot," I respond.

"Good riot or bad riot?" Nell stops, tongs in midair, studying me—not suspiciously, but in a curious way. "Who did you come to the party with?"

"I'm homeschooling Micah and Dula at the Flannigan ranch."

Instantly, Nell's face and tongs droop. "Those precious little nuggets—God bless 'em." She dabs at her eyes. "CeCe Flannigan was a good woman. You take good care of her little ones, OK?"

I nod. Micah and Dula's mother must have been amazing to illicit such praise from the kitchen help.

"Oh, hello, Mick! Hope and I were just talking about CeCe."

My boss, Michael Flannigan, grabs Nell in a bear hug and lifts her off her feet. Another man their age wrestles Nell out of Mr. Flannigan's arms and lays a sloppy wet kiss on her mouth to stop her squealing. "Hope, hurry! Get me another spoon!" she says, breathless.

I flush and stutter. Nell notices how uncomfortable I am.

"Mort, put me down. Hope, since your boss and this lug are being rude, let me introduce you to my husband, Mortimer Findley, the padrone of this ranch."

"Nellie Lister, don't lie to the girl. It's *your* ranch—all gabillion acres of it." To keep her from squirming away from the truth, her husband has locked his arms around her.

"Unlike what her daddy thought," he says to me, "I didn't give two hoots about her land. I married her for her body!" He releases his wife, and she scurries to the other side of the center island.

"The *Lister* Ranch?" I say, totally confused.

"Yes," they say in unison.

"Lister is my maiden name." Nell is obviously embarrassed. "Now, let's stop all this fuss and go dance." She struts toward the door.

I want to crawl under the kitchen table. This woman is Janelle Lister—the only offspring of Beauregard Lister. Even *I* know who he is. Why would a woman who owns untold thousands of acres be slaving away in the kitchen at her own party?

"Honey?" Mort attempts to slow his wife down long enough to tuck her flyaway hair back into the haphazard bun. She ducks to avoid him.

"We hired half of Encinal to cater this party." He reaches toward her again, looking clumsy and sweet.

"They're so young, Morty. You remember how it used to be?" Nell touches her husband's face.

"Once they set up the food, I told them they could go enjoy the party and check on things now and then. You know I don't mind being in the kitchen."

"Don't you mean *hiding* in the kitchen?"

Michael Flannigan chuckles at his friends and looks out the window. I panic, remembering the children.

"I'd better go check on Dula and Micah," I say.

Michael Flannigan smiles. "Don't worry, Hope. The kids are with their cousin having a blast. I'm glad you met these folks. Nell is a very special lady—so good to my CeCe in her last months." He joins his friends and leaves me alone with my bucket of feelings.

There is an industrial-sized coffee pot in the corner of the kitchen. I'm already overstimulated and off-center by the chaotic energy, but I still need something to hold in my hands. The cabinet behind the coffee cups is filled with a forest of bottles—an assortment of liquor and sherry for cooking. Jeez!

"Face it, Hope," I say to myself. "You can't escape."

TWENTY-THREE

FOR SOME REASON, MY MOOD IS QUITE JOLLY THIS MORNING. THE beauty of creation screams from every rock and bush—in a good way. With eyes closed, I breathe in the subtle and dusty fragrances and watch the wind dance with the dust. I came home from the party, fell asleep in a strange position, and woke up with my hip out of whack, and I still don't feel cranky. What is the *deal*? This could be a miracle.

Maybe communicating with Oz-God does change things, even if it's only in my imagination. I'm not sure, but I think it was Carl Jung who said that true transformation happens through story, myth, and image, not with distant mental concepts. I really don't care if this experience is a so-called myth, I *feel* it. Must I have an affidavit to prove it to anyone else?

All my life I've looked for a relationship with someone who might give me love and comfort, but since Steve, I question my perception of happiness. Me finding a soulmate here on Earth? Only on the Hallmark channel ...

"Deep thoughts."

"Are you going to sue me from some heavenly realm?"

"What's different today?"

"I think I must have accidentally sleepwalked into a parallel existence. There are other dimensions, right?"

"More than you can imagine."

"Everywhere I look I see a haiku. Actually, just forget I said that."

"Did you have a nice time last night?"

"I didn't drink."

"That isn't what I asked."

"Let's talk about something else."

"Turkey vultures?"

"You know, a few drops of rain out here could do wonders. There are probably millions of dormant flower seeds buried like treasures in the ground."

"I also know that there were some interesting treasures at the party."

"You better not be talking about men. Besides, you already know everything."

"It's much better when you share your life voluntarily."

"Here's a question—what happens if someone decides to avoid men altogether?"

"Is that what you want?"

"Relationships don't turn out very well for me."

"Rain can transform the desert."

"Cheater … I just said that."

"Aren't you attempting to collapse old ways of thinking?"

"Why change if there is no one to love?"

"Relationships take faith and trust. Besides, you don't need a man to be happy."

"Good, because I'm finished trusting men."

"There is always risk involved."

"My biggest risk so far is talking to you."

"I will never leave you."

"Prove it."

"You'll see …"

"When?"

"Tell me as story about the desert and the rain."

"You only do this to humiliate me."

"Not so! Pretty please?"

"I feel that I'm back in Mrs. Hoover's first grade class."

"Attention, everyone! Hope will now explain the metaphor of the desert and the rain."

"You asked for it."

"Can't wait."

"Well, Dick dumped Jane for some other skank. Soon, after listening to the voices in her head, Jane flipped out and climbed up the hill with a bottle of bourbon and danced with the devil. After tumbling down into the pit of hell, she was imprisoned and banished to the desert … believing that if she shed enough tears and survived this terrible season of punishment, she might earn another chance to bloom."

"OK, maybe this wasn't such a good idea."

"Are you criticizing my story?"

"Desert time isn't punishment."

"Are you telling me I don't know *Dick?*"

"Or squat."

"This is probably an inappropriate question, but do any of you ghost types laugh at dirty jokes?"

"Being inappropriate is part of your process."

"Kind of vague and weaselly …"

"First tell me why you feel better this morning."

"Make me."

"Feeling upbeat is usually a foreign concept for you."

"All right, here is a better rendition of the story. I'm beginning to see that the desert might be a gift—a place to wrestle with my demons. You, Oz-God, are both the dryness and the rain, which come at different times for the transformation of my character into the original blueprint on my puzzle box. When the healing rains fall, it's a blooming miracle."

"I'm speechless."

"May I sit down, Mrs. Hoover?"

"Look, your behavior chart is peppered with stars!"

"When you speak of *process,* you mean it in a multifaceted, godlike way, right?"

"Google it."

"'Process, verb: to prepare, refine, smelt, distill, extract, convert, transform.' Yep, sounds painful."

"Process and pain both begin with the same letter … By the way, the answer is yes."

"Yes, what?"

"We laugh at your jokes."

TWENTY-FOUR

THE SCENT OF HORSE MANURE, HAY, AND LEATHER WAFTS toward me from the barn. Plink, plink, plink ... Must be Manuel. Today the horses will wear new shoes. Someone in the barn is singing a Spanish love song. I must investigate.

"Whoa, Bonita!" The ranch hand/farrier holds tightly to the hind leg of a brown-and-white mare as he eyeballs her hoof for the right-sized shoe. From underneath the horse's belly, he says to me, "Let her smell your perfume. It will calm her."

"I'm not wearing perfume," I say.

The man lets the hoof drop with a thud and stands up, looking at me as he strokes the horse's back. His gray-flecked eyebrows rise as if we are actors in a spaghetti western and I've forgotten my lines, but his black eyes are kind, almost disappearing into nests of brown wrinkles.

"Oh, you don't mean *actual* perfume. Just me, my scent." I blush and move toward the mare's head, sticking my hand out. Her soft nose touches my fingers lightly, and she opens her lips as if to take a nibble. I yank my hand away, making the horse toss her head and snort.

"Oh, I'm sorry. Horses scare me a little."

The farrier laughs and picks up another leg, holding the mare's ankle securely before prying the old, worn horseshoe away from the ragged hoof. His hands are scarred and seem to work independently from his thoughts.

"She is jealous ... want's me all to herself. Don't you, Bonita?"

"I always wanted to ride a horse."

"Jack hasn't taken the lovely senorita for a ride?" He smiles.

"I haven't met Jack yet. By the way, I'm Hope. I teach the children."

"*Si, Esperanza. Yo soy Manuel.*"

"I don't speak Spanish, but I'm very glad to meet you."

"Are you an angel, Esperanza? Have you come to bring something wonderful into our lives?" he asks. I assume he is teasing me.

"I doubt that. I think I'll just focus on not burning something down," I say, and we both laugh. "What does the name, Manuel, mean?"

"In English, my name is Emmanuel." He shrugs and moves to the mare's front hooves. She whinnies and tosses her head again until he speaks soothing words.

"Shh, shh, Bonita. You don't have to be afraid."

He looks straight at me as he reassures the animal. I suddenly want to be somewhere else. His words feel heavy, encoded with a double meaning.

"What has made you so *irritado*?" he says suddenly.

I giggle nervously. "Does that mean angry? I'm not angry, just afraid of horses." (Why is he asking personal questions and making me uncomfortable?) With hands in my back pockets, I look toward the other stalls where four sets of long-lashed horse eyes stare at me.

Manuel laughs, the kind that comes from a deep and secret place. "My sister Marcella says I am pushy and should act with more respect." His words only soothe my indignation for a nanosecond.

"You must admit, *senorita,* anger burns the soul like poison. Even the horse, she feels your pain. Revenge is for God alone."

"You're right. I'm angry and afraid of just about everything. So what?" The moment I admit it, the horse calms down. Two tears leak out and roll down my cheeks. I look away quickly, forcing my expression to remain stony. "Life isn't fair. I don't know what I've done to deserve all this."

"Que?"

"Why should evil people get away with everything? Don't I have a right to demand justice for my … my injuries?" My voice sounds squeaky and young. "Your sister is right. You *are* pushy. I don't even know you. You have no right to pry into my life. I have no idea why I'm telling you these things."

"Because I'm just a harmless Mexican laborer?" Manuel smiles at me in a sly way.

"Of course not! I didn't mean it that way … I'm *not* prejudiced against anyone!"

Manuel hammers a horseshoe onto the newly filed hoof, and I feel a wave of nausea at how close the nails are to the quick.

"God's wrath is more than punishment—it comes from the fiercest love." Using a sharp, curved tool, he begins to pare away the old and cracked part of another hoof.

"What do you mean? Righteous judgment sends sinners straight to hell." (Where did that catechism-o'-nine-tails come from?)

"Oh, no, Little Esperanza." He takes some of the hoof shavings and tosses them to the dogs by the barn door. "El Senor will do anything to save us. He does not hate like we do but loves us with a vengeance, like a child, who must learn. We make choices and the world answers." Manuel spanks one hand against the back of the other, careful not to startle the horse.

"The people who have hurt me deserve more than a spanking."

"Hm. And what, *mi tesoro*, do you deserve?"

TWENTY-FIVE

FTER MY TIME IN THE BARN, I'M UNABLE TO SIT STILL. HURRY. Clean the house. Smile. Don't let anyone see my blood burning. My thoughts are crunchy bugs pinned alive to cardboard. Oh, how they squirm.

The opportunity to babysit Micah and Dula at the pool arises. What a relief. I'm calmed by their innocence and lack of self-consciousness. They think I'm asleep behind my sunglasses, and I watch their thin, slick bodies move through the water like seals. Am I a freak for finding so much joy in watching them?

I need to deal with my issues, but I feel handcuffed, as if forced to write my life story with a pencil in my teeth. Am I full of rage like Manuel said? Are bitterness and shame so ingrained into the foundations of my personality that I no longer notice?

Horrible things happened to me when I was a child. How do I get over that? The Universe has dropped me naked into my own reality show. Deliver me from evil …

The sun burns my exposed skin, probably encouraging dormant melanoma cells to wake up. Human flesh, while flexible and aesthetically awe-inspiring, is no different from any other meat on the planet. I look down at my freckled thighs. Every day my body rots a little more.

"There she is, the Hope we know and love …"

"Just facing reality, Oz-God."

"How can you look at those precious children and not have faith in the future?"

"Are all children born knowing about your invisible world?"

"Why don't you ask them?"

"I'll bet you want us to dumb down and be like them, so we are easier to control."

"You think children are dumb? They arrive perfect and still remember where they came from."

"And then our parents beat it out of us."

"Childlike is different from childish. It's about recognizing truth and reconnecting to Source."

"Marco!" Micah yells. He is peeking through his fingers. Dula barely whispers, *"Polo,"* and runs around the pool to stand beside me. Wrapping her in a towel, I pull her into my arms. She is shivering.

"Hey, no fair!" Micah slaps the water with his hand.

"You cheated," Dula whines. "I don't want to play anymore." She leans her wet head against my chest and her thumb slips into her mouth.

As I rock her, she drifts into sleep—a perfect moment.

"Oz-God?"

"You rang?"

"Is there a difference between soul and spirit?"

"Soul is part of your human nature."

"Like a record of the things I've experienced?"

"Your resume."

"How is soul different from spirit?"

"Spirit is the eternal part that carries your particular frequency signature from Source."

"I'm not sure I get the difference."

"It's possible to succeed in life, be a decent, charitable person, and never choose to activate the sliver of Spirit where I live."

"So, someone can have a good soul record without being spiritually awakened?"

"Activating your God gene is a freewill choice."

"Or I can choose to stay in denial. Is there no peace for the wicked?"

"Unconditional love is the most powerful energy there is and can transform anything."

"Define *anything*."

"Every molecule of creation carries a fractal of creative source—all is connected."

"What about now? Paradigms in science, religion, and metaphysics are shifting. Doesn't that affect religion and our understanding of God and the Universe?"

"Hope?"

"Am I in trouble?"

"You rock …"

"You may want to withhold your opinion. I'm not finished."

"I'm counting on it."

"So far, we've established that thoughts, actions, and emotions are a part of my soul/flesh, which tends to run amok."

"It's the nature of undisciplined flesh."

"How am I supposed to know what's broken? I mean, besides the obvious …"

"The obvious is a perfect place to start. Prayer and meditation help."

"Did you say meditation or medication?"

TWENTY-SIX

O N THE GROUND BESIDE ME IS A TINY DEAD FIELD MOUSE, mummified and flat like a crispy tortilla chip. My breath feels hot. Wouldn't it be interesting if we all began to measure time in breaths? "I'll pick you up in about three hundred breaths!" Then we'd really have to pay attention to the moment.

I sit on the porch swing breathing—sucking in environmental molecules, dust from the road, and particles of dead mouse and then absorbing them into my body. What about my past? Did I simply breathe in my family dysfunction? If only I could have said, "Mom and Dad? Keep your freaking shitty particles to yourself!"

I know who I am in this state, even if everything is broken.

"Rationalization is such a lovely shade of putrid."

"You're not helping, Oz-God."

"I know you want to find true love."

"Like I could possibly care about men right now!"

"Ya never know. Besides, love isn't just about men."

"I've never trusted anyone really—man or woman."

"You don't necessarily believe in me either, and yet, here we are."

"I think underneath it all, alcohol was what ruined my marriage."

"Did you drink before?"

"Well, yes ... I was stealing vodka from my parents in sixth grade."

"Addiction is a good place for you to start, so are childhood traumas."

"Start what?"

"The scavenger hunt."

"What if I don't want to work that hard?"

"The last time you ignored your spiritual quest, you ended up in jail."

"There is that."

"Or, you are free to reject all of it, lock me back in the closet."

"Glad we're on the same page."

"However, evolution doesn't happen without some writhing around in the muck."

"I hate muck."

"You seem surprised that some effort on your part is required."

"You won't expect me to be perfect?"

"Lots of room on this ranch to thrash about and look foolish."

"I'm afraid."

"No one is watching."

"I don't suppose issues ever disappear on their own, do they?"

TWENTY-SEVEN

"MARCELLA?" THE KITCHEN DOOR IS OPEN. I PUSH ON THE screen, feeling like an intruder. "It's Hope. Have you seen the children?"

"Come in," she says.

As far as I can tell, Marcella cooks for the family and takes care of Dula and Micah when they aren't with me. She is a tall woman of mixed blood, very different from the other employees at World's End. She wears beautiful silver jewelry and artistic clothing—must be a story there.

She is standing in the middle of the kitchen facing a young man at least a foot taller than she is. They turn their heads at the same time, and I see the resemblance.

"Hope, this is my son, Jack."

I try to avoid staring. This must be the shadowy Junior that Fred was referring to. I recognize his well-fitting jeans from the party.

"I bet everyone comments on your name." Jack's smile reaches his eyes, which are greenish brown and have a nice sparkle. Bonus. No, stop. Attractive man. Turn around and run like the wind.

"Dulita left you a note at the windmill. She and Micah have been working all morning on an adventure for you." Marcella lifts the lid on a huge Dutch oven and stirs, releasing a tempting fragrance of onion and red chilies. My stomach rumbles.

"There will be guests for dinner. I believe you know the Findleys. Please join us." Marcella is kind to include me in the house-family.

"OK, thanks. Nice to meet you, Jack."

"Ciao," he says to my back.

Ciao? That's Italian, not Spanish. Oh well. Not my problem.

The path—more like an overgrown cow track—starts behind a vast and metal-roofed pole barn that houses a conglomeration of World War II army trucks and other ancient ranch vehicles. There are so many parts missing, exchanged, or welded to each other that I half expect Igor to lurch around the corner and screech, "They're *alive!*"

"Somebody's got a hobby ..." I immediately think of Jack shirtless and wearing a tool belt. Whoa there, chica. What is wrong with me? Is my first reaction to objectify men? How does that make me any different that the sexist pigs I love to judge?

Shaking my head, I paw through an assortment of rusted iron tools stacked haphazardly on a dilapidated wooden worktable. No stainless steel machete, Dang! This stuff is *old.* Finally, I hook a hammer through my belt loop ... Why? In case of a zombie apocalypse? I feel very unbalanced.

Today is already too hot. No breeze. Not even the windmill blades do anything more than rattle and creak. The cacti look flat and dehydrated. I'm wearing tennis shoes and shorts; I just can't stand jeans when the weather is sweltering.

A hornet has already stung my arm today. I pick up the pace, flapping and slapping as I go. Give me sharks and jellyfish any day.

The Flannigans call this section of their land The Trap. The grass rustles. I must have startled a coyote—its bushy brown tail flashes at me through the tall grass. The pack is probably surrounding me now, planning a way to take down the city girl.

In the middle of the path is an explosion. Judging by the size and white tips of some of the longer feathers, I assume a Mexican eagle gave up the ghost last night. Footprints of all kinds surround the mess—evidence of nocturnal creatures participating in the grizzly social event.

I never realized that silence is a sound. More than a buzz or hum, it presses in like an invisible presence against my temples producing a slow, deep throb that aligns with my pulse. Because of Oz-God,

I know that silence isn't empty. Could this be the sound of creation breathing?

Micah and Dula have planned a surprise for me. I smile. Should they be out here by themselves? A large and noisy insect jumps out of the grass, clacking its wings together. "Jeezus!" I'm such a weenie.

The note flapping from a bush on blue flowered paper is rolled up with a string like a cigar. The other end of the string disappears into the bushes. I read:

> Roses are red
> Hope is blue
> Follow the string
> Don't let anything eat you!

Micah knows I'm afraid of javelina ... well, all the wild beasts. If this is Micah and Dula's version of a wilderness survival test. I will follow this string no matter where it leads. Good Lord, do I have to crawl under that? Humph ... the little darlings.

If I come to the end of this string and get lost in a tangle of thorns ... Is that a giggle? Carefully, I peek through the bushes and see a flash of red. If I sneak around them in a wide circle, I can scare them from behind. Creeping quietly, like a Navajo warrior, I see their small backs. I will couch down over here and ...

I hear the rattle a moment before the snake sinks its fangs into my thigh. I scream and fall to my knees, trying to scramble away. My leg is on fire. Must keep the children away.

"Stop, Micah, rattlesnake!" I feel faint.

Too dizzy ... Dula's high, thin scream. A thud. Micah drops a rock on the snake and picks up a hammer. Did I drop it? Try not to pass out.

The snake is trapped, thrashing its tail. Micah pounds the head to a pulp, but the body still whips back and forth; the sound of the rattle ... My throat and lips swell, and I feel the poison crawling through my body like blistering death.

"Micah ... Go get help!"

What seems like centuries later, Marcella's worried face hovers over mine while other strong arms carry me. My whole body feels numb. Wind, noise, and dirt sting my face. I hear the rhythmic pounding of helicopter blades ... Where are they taking me?

Green eyes close to my face—angel eyes.

"Am I going to die?" My voice sounds muffled.

I can't hear his response but see his head shake and his lips form a word: "No." He doesn't seem sure.

Maybe heaven is around the corner. Forgive me ...

TWENTY-EIGHT

MY BED IS A TOMB. DEMON DUST CREEPS UNDER THE DOOR. My body throbs with pain as familiar anxiety rises to the top—poison on top of poison. Oh, yes, the snake ... Yet, I'm still alive. Thank you ...

Marcella's warm hands seem to be imbued with the healing of the Ancient Ones—smoothing my hair and speaking soft words that I don't understand. Grief and gratefulness seep out and wet my pillow.

"Who is that man sitting by the door?" I ask.

"Remember my son, Jack?" she says. "He saved you."

I remember and shut my eyes, listening to mother and son whisper in the candlelight.

"Jack, why are you still here?" she asks him.

"I'm not sure, *Mamacita*. Just making sure she ..." Jack hesitates as his mother holds a warm teacup to my lips.

The candle flame flickers over the planes of their faces, angular and beautiful.

"Is that creosote tea?" he asks, a shudder in his voice.

"It will help bring the fever down and clean the poison out of her body," she says.

"Does Hope know who we are, or does she think we're the help?" Jack's voice sounds far away, and I must fight to listen.

"Why are you worried about what she thinks?" Marcella hisses. "Are you ever going to stop fighting, *mijo*?"

"I'm so tired of people looking down on us."

"You are healthy, rich, and have much education, yet sometimes you act as if we swam across the Rio Grande in the middle of the night and have no right to be here."

"You didn't grow up here, Mama. You don't know what it's like to be born into white privilege but also have roots in your Hispanic heritage."

"You should be proud to walk in both worlds."

"The world is still ignorant in so many ways."

"You were born in America to a legally married couple named Flanagan. Our light Spanish skin is whiter than most of the people on this ranch. The fact that I grew up in Mexico is no different that moving here from Italy."

"Oh, Mama … If only that were true." Jack's boots make a scuffle as he rises to his feet. "I need some air."

He is sad … and gone. The room feels empty. I'm even more confused. My precious matchstick kingdom is falling, and my limited perception of reality, exposed. I slide back into oblivion.

In my dreams, I drink wine to calm my broken heart. In this shadowy world, the fruit of the vine doesn't betray me, but how do I silence the crying baby?

TWENTY-NINE

SOFT MORNING LIGHT FILTERS THROUGH THE LACY CURTAINS. Have I been here two days? Three? The pain in my leg is much better, but the knot in my chest won't budge.

"Why a snake? Oz-God, what am I doing wrong?"

"Good morning, Bonita." Marcella walks in with a teacup and toast. "Who is Oz-God?"

"Did I say something out loud?" I struggle to sit up in bed, trying to look less like an invalid.

Marcella sets the tray down and begins straightening the room. "You know"—she pauses, folding a towel—"your snakebite was not punishment from God. Snakebite is the signature of el diablo."

"How do you know this?"

She smiles, and I remember that Manuel is her brother.

"Wasn't it convenient that Jack was here to carry you?"

"Yes, you're right."

"You think it is coincidence that the border patrol just happened to have rattlesnake antivenom?"

"You're right. I'm ungrateful and full of self-pity."

The woman's silver braid tickles my arm as she removes the bandage on my leg and cleans the inflamed skin with something that stings and smells like camphor.

"What is the pay day?" Marcella asks.

"Excuse me?"

"For your self-pity. You feel better after?"

Marcella hands me a box of tissues; my rebellious eyes have overflowed again. "*Calma*, my sweet. You aren't alone anymore." She picks up a brush and gently picks at the tangles in my hair.

"What does *Bonita* mean?" I ask.

"It means, beautiful."

"Manuel called me that."

"My brother and I invite you out of the darkness."

"Where did you come from? Do you work here? I don't understand what's happening. Everything feels mixed up. If the snake bite isn't punishment for my sins, then ..."

"Shh, Bonita. Sleep now."

THIRTY

I HAVE BEEN SENT INTO THE YARD WITH MARCELLA'S KNEE-HIGH, snake-proof boots, tongs, gloves, and a galvanized bucket to pluck pear apples off the cacti so Marcella can make jelly. I feel woozy. It's my first time up for any length of time.

Pear plucking is a challenge. South Texas cacti have pancake-shaped pads and sometimes grow into six-foot bushes. Each pad has two or three pears, sometimes more, and the color ... bright magenta. I wish I had lipstick this color.

Tufts of hairlike prickles manage to sneak under my gloves. I seek the almost invisible thorns with my tongue, nibbling at them with my teeth.

"How do you like my necklace?" Micah is keeping a close eye on me since I left the house—my personal bodyguard. He shakes the impressive set of rattles in my face, and I almost drop the bucket.

"*Micah,* you little sh ... stinker! Do that again, and I'll kiss your face!"

"OK, I give! You want to see the snakeskin? I scraped the meat off with an arrowhead, rubbed it with salt, and stretched it on a board with nails. Five and a half feet—a real beaut!"

Did the sun just get about twenty degrees hotter?

"Maybe I'll take a look after lunch."

I think of the soup I saw Marcella preparing earlier. People don't really eat rattlesnakes, do they? Could be some shamanic ritual she is preparing for me. I must focus on my task. Grab the purple pear with the tongs, twist, and drop it in the bucket. Repeat.

"I've never been snakebit before." Micah sounds disappointed.

"They wouldn't dare bite a fearless snake-skinner like you …"

"Yeah, I'd beat his head in."

"You'll be my hero forever." I grab the bill of his cap with my tongs and lift it off his head.

"Hey, gimme that!"

"Only if you go play somewhere else. I don't need a babysitter."

"But Marcella *said*—"

"You want to spend all day picking thorns out of this cap?" I say, dangling it over some cactus.

"OK, OK!" Micah must come near me to grab it—I swiftly kiss his cheek. He blushes and makes a motion to wipe it off, but a grin betrays him.

"Don't blame me if you die," he says, whacking his cap on his leg as if removing my cooties.

I can eat snake if I have to. This is the fricking desert, and I must survive. If I eat the flesh of my enemy, I possess its power, right?

"Look at you out here fearlessly romping in the bushes." Jack knows how to creep like a silent warrior. Maybe he can teach me some things.

I jump and threaten him with my tongs.

"Having a little hair of the snake?"

"You're as bad as Micah. Besides, snakes don't have hair. They have huge fangs filled with nasty chemicals that have probably given me brain damage," I say, turning my back toward him.

"Thoughts are chemicals too, you know." Jack spears a pear-apple with a stick and scrapes it into my bucket.

"Are you comparing my thoughts to snake venom?"

(Why do I flirt with absolutely every man in the universe? I know he is only taking over babysitting duty for Micah, and yet …)

"I googled you," he adds casually.

"What? Why?" I say, flattered and embarrassed at the same time.

"I often research interesting subjects." This time, Jack has speared three pears on his stick like a kebob.

"And do you always help your mother with the jelly?"

He throws the stick like a spear. "Not since I was Micah's age."

(Men are so endearing and annoying when they strut.)

"You're pretty impressive on paper, young lady: psychology, published papers on neurons ..."

"I traded psychology for the ambiguities of philosophy years ago. Besides, I'm sure you know the story of why I'm down on this ranch, right? Ouch!" A large thorn pokes through my jeans.

"That story is also interesting. Here, let me. I'm a pro at thorn extraction."

"Well, this is a first," I say, throwing another pear so hard into the bucket that it bounces out.

"What's a first?"

"To have someone say that drunk and disorderly are interesting!"

"Nobody told me that part," Jack says, grinning.

"Great. Nothing like another dose of humiliation!"

"Just kidding. I know," he says. "We have more in common than you think."

"I doubt it."

"I took psychology in college. Does that count?"

"What else did you study?" I ask, relieved that we are off the subject of me.

"I have a masters in ranch management."

(Strut, strut, strut.)

"And yes," he continues as if reading my mind. "I've been trying to find a subtle way to work that piece of information into the conversation."

"Why?"

"Because you think I'm a dumb cowboy."

"I do not."

"And, for the record, I'm also sort of bad at this small talk thing."

Just like Micah, Jack hits his hat on his leg and returns it to his head, lips pressed together.

(Danger, danger.)

"Well, Mr. Big Stuff, if you googled my published paper, you must remember the way neurons function in the brain?"

"Now who's showing off?! Of course I remember." Jack puts his hand over his heart as if in pain. "Is this a test?"

"Maybe." I turn away so he can't see me blush.

"Let's see … Neurons fire and release neurotransmitters along certain set of circuits, painting a chemical picture of a thought or experience. Something like that?"

"Very good!"

He continues, "Through time and repetition, a thought becomes a chemical pathway."

"Did you memorize the paper, or what?"

"No. It was very intriguing, though—made me think about my father." Jack's voice sounds tight.

"Do I dare ask why?"

"I started wondering if every time my father got drunk and told me I was stupid if a surge of shitty chemicals raced around my brain creating a dysfunctional road map."

"That's quite a personal revelation …" I say quietly.

"Now we're even."

"I get the feeling you don't normally talk about your father."

Jack stares at me. "Were you awake when my mom and I were whispering in your room?"

"I heard bits and pieces but was hallucinating at the time, so …"

We fall silent, but I don't feel uncomfortable.

"You know," I say, changing the subject, "not only do all those toxic chemicals become hardwired into our personalities, but they also burn up good neurotransmitters like serotonin at an alarming rate. Thank God for antidepressants."

"Why did I have to bring up this subject?" He laughs. "It's what I get for trying to impress you."

"Would it help if I told you it worked?"

"Right, you're impressed that I'm still living in an illusion based on the memories of my paternal shit show?" he asks in mock horror.

We both start laughing—then I stop. His words pierce my own denial.

"Oh wow. I just realized something," I say.

"What?"

"I wrote that paper years ago and never fully applied it to my own experience."

"Maybe that's why so many psychologists become sicko serial killers."

"I'm not a psychologist. I teach philosophy—at least I used to," I say, still dazed.

"Pardon *me*! I just hang out here with the cows and horses."

"You know what this means, don't you?"

"I have no idea," Jack says, interested.

"The brain doesn't differentiate between reality and memories," I explain.

"OK ... and?" Jack scans my face intently.

"The perpetuation of the shit show, as you described it, continues because we are releasing the same destructive chemicals in our brains every time we replay what our fathers ... uh, what happened in our pasts."

I bend over, unable to catch my breath.

Jack looks worried. "Hey, Hope, let's get some iced tea before our heads blow up." He takes my tongs and bucket and starts walking me toward the ranch house.

Did he and I just have this conversation? What the hell is happening?

THIRTY-ONE

A s I OPEN THE DOOR TO MY ADOBE, AN OWL BROADCASTS ITS repetitive question down the chimney. *Whoo? Whoo? Whoo?* Who, indeed ...

I'm glad to be back in my own place. My down comforter lies crooked across the bed, and three-day-old lunch dishes are still in the sink. A film of forgetfulness has settled over my belongings.

Incandescent bulbs seem too harsh tonight. Striking a wooden match, I light a few of the tall, religious candles that fill a cabinet in the kitchen. St. Joseph, the Virgin of Guadalupe, and Jesus of the Sacred Heart surround my living room with flickering shadows—protection.

The whitewashed walls are like a cave—smooth and silent. Come, Spirit ... Transform the refuse of my life. If I'm unable to forgive my own weakness, how can I love or forgive someone else? I know the names of some of my demons. Why can't I let them go?

Jesus on the candle is wearing his physical heart on the outside of his clothes. It looks anatomically correct. His eyes are full of compassion. Forgive me, Father, for I have sinned. Forgive my father, for he sinned against me.

"Forgiveness is a different kind of beast—not a stray you feed once and then shoo away from the back door."

"Then what, Oz-God? No one seems to be able to tell me how to move forward."

"Sometimes the stray returns a million times. You forgive, wander back into resentment, return your eyes to the flame, and forgive again. The candle burns; the wax disappears ... process."

"So forgiveness isn't something that happens to you but a choice that you make again and again?"

"It's cozy in here ... safe."

"Maybe every time I choose to forgive, one thorny pear apple thuds into the bucket? So far, my bucket feels empty."

"I don't know. Looks like you and Jack were gathering something today."

"Why are you so patient with me?"

"Love is patient."

"The people on this ranch are being nice. I don't like it."

"Not even Jack?"

"Nice try, pushy pants."

"Just a simple question."

"Nothing is simple when it comes to you."

"What did you say about your empty bucket?"

"I don't trust love, patience, or forgiveness. My days of starvation will return soon enough."

"Is that your choice?"

"I'm a victim to my chemicals."

"Truth has a different set of chemicals."

"Whose truth? Yours? You know I don't follow the rules."

"Our ways are different from yours ... quantum. More amazing than you can imagine right now."

"And we're back where we started."

THIRTY-TWO

OPEN THE FRONT DOOR AND INVITE THE NIGHT AIR INTO MY candlelit grotto. The moon looks like one of Dula's sparkle stickers on a black velvet curtain. I want to walk. Do I dare? I still have Marcella's snake-proof boots.

Not far down the wide caliche road between my adobe and the barn, there is a hidden dump. Old refrigerators, washing machines, and rusted-out hot water heaters stand in a circle casting shadows in the moonlight like a south Texas Stonehenge. Creosote bushes release their aroma into the night, reminding me of Marcella's healing tea.

Sitting on an upside-down chest freezer, I listen. The desert cranks out night noises like a factory. Coyotes howl, and my heart pumps. I send out a psychic blast to everything and everyone within a ten-mile radius—snakes, coyotes, and illegal aliens, beware.

Manuel's tune reaches out to me like a birthday hug. He walks straight toward me, so I won't be startled, and hops up next to me on the freezer. His knees creak. Backlit by the moon, all I can see is his silhouette and a blaze of white teeth. His shirt smells like tobacco— not the cheap, papery smell of store-bought cigarettes but the kind of tobacco that comes in a pouch.

"How did you know I was out here?"

"It's nighttime. We worry." He kicks the heel of his boot gently against the freezer, making a deep and hollow sound. "I told Marcella you were fine—had joined the brotherhood of the snake, and its power was in your veins."

"Stop it."

"I believe it to be true, but I believe many things."

"Like what?"

"That our ancestors are out there." He points to the stars.

"No shit? Me too."

"I also hear the Coyote whisper." Manuel's voice drops in reverence.

"Coyote?"

"He has many names ..."

"What does Coyote whisper?" I ask.

Manuel pauses for dramatic effect.

"You are full of bull, Grandpa." I elbow him in the ribs so I can hear his deep laugh.

"Coyote says your scent has attracted a tall cowboy animal ... much more dangerous than the snake." Manuel elbows me back.

"Well, you tell *Coyote* I can handle any two-legged varmint that comes along."

"I slide to the ground, making sure to land on my good leg. "You and Marcella treat me like a baby who can't find her way home."

He pats my hand. "Oh, no. Coyote says you have a treasure map."

THIRTY-THREE

"YOUR UNCLE WARNED ME ABOUT YOU, JACK." THERE IS AN awkward silence as we drive out the main gate. I'm nervous to be alone with him.

"Uncle Manny is ... eccentric. No tellin' what he'll say." He reaches over and touches my knee. "Does your leg still hurt?"

I have been clasping my hands in my lap, virtually holding my breath.

"No, the leg is fine. I'm just agitated for some reason ... must be the idea of going to an AA meeting. I haven't been much since my relapse."

"I tried staying sober on my own," he says. "Failed both times. I hate admitting that I need anyone else, you know. It has taken three tries to gather a few consecutive years together."

"You could have mentioned that you were in the program the last time we talked."

Jack laughs. "Yeah, I suppose I could have. How about that conversation ... Weird, huh? I hope you don't think I'm too strange."

"I'm the one who freaked out ... haven't had a conversation like that in a while." I turn and look out the window.

Outside the truck window, the landscape looks scorched. Clouds of powdered earth billow behind the truck, blanketing the brush beside the road.

"Most men I know aren't interested in the way the mind works, much less want to discuss it with a woman."

"You're a professor. There must be intelligent guys everywhere."

"I said men, not academics ... big difference."

"Was that a compliment?" Jack slides me a glance, and I smile.

"This ranch is really beautiful—in a desiccated mouse-mummy sort of way."

"Now who's the subject changer? Desiccated mouse mummy? What the heck?"

I can feel Jack watching me. "You know, dehydrated ... desert like beauty? Look at those." I point. In the distance, two small funnel clouds of dust twirl across the flat land.

"Dula loves running after the dust devils." Jacks smile is soft. "One knocked her down once, but that didn't stop her."

"I know how she feels ... the knocking down part, at least."

Jack turns on music from a playlist on his phone, and we relax. I smile at how many of the tunes are also on my favorites list. Another coincidence? (I'm so pitiful.)

In the bank drive-through, Jack pulls a check from his wallet. I try not to watch but see his name printed on the top of it: Jack P. Flannigan Jr.

"So you're actually Micah and Dula's cousin?" I ask.

He takes a deep breath and looks at me without answering, endorses a few checks, and puts all of it in the teller's drawer.

"The age difference is so big that uncle sounds better."

"So, your dad is Michael Flannigan's brother?"

"Is that so hard to believe?" A dark look crosses his face. "Did you think my mother was just a maid for the Flannigan household?"

"No, I ..."

"Just because I look Hispanic and work on the ranch ... Oh, forget it."

I'm stunned into silence by his anger-fueled words.

"I'm just so sick of trying to prove myself to everyone." I can see his jaw flexing as he continues. "I'm smart. I lived in Europe. I have patents on three inventions, and people still think I'm a stupid ..."

Jack looks over at me and blushes almost purple. "Gee, guess that's been building up a while. Sorry. Obviously, I have a few issues."

The fact that he has said the word *issues* makes me feel warm and toasty inside.

"If you want to say the f-word or something, I don't mind," I say.

Now he is surprised and grins.

I continue. "Sometimes I get the urge to yell it out, but I'm trying to be polite."

Jack laughs. "Well, if you yell fuck at this AA meeting, they will just think you'd spilled your coffee and tell you to keep coming back." He smiles and then knits his brows together. "What makes you want to yell the f-word?"

"You have to *ask*? Sobriety is so … I don't know, cruel and *unnatural*."

"I'll tell you what's unnatural," Jack says, making a right turn into a parking lot where I assume the meeting will be. "Pizza without a beer."

Bingo.

THIRTY-FOUR

BLOW ON MY STEAMING MOCHA FRAPPÉ IN THE AIR-CONDITIONED Starbucks, watching Jack devour an orange and cranberry scone in two bites. I almost comment but don't want to be critical at this stage of our relationship. Relationship? Whatever.

"I must admit being in a room full of screwed-up people like me is such a relief. Does that make me a freak?" Jack asks.

"Everyone is messed up, you know—not just alcoholics." I sound like a school marm.

"Yeah, but we have to admit it before spouting advice. Most ranchers don't understand alcoholism at all," Jack says. "They don't trust a man who won't drink."

"Had some personal experience with that?"

Jack leans back on two legs of his chair. "Don't get me started on the good-ole'-boy code around here."

"Personally, if someone admits to me that they are in *any* recovery program, it makes me trust them more," I say, trying not to spew any crumbs.

"Oh, yeah? Why?" Jack settles his chair back on the floor and leans toward me. I can smell the fresh scent of his laundry detergent. I wonder if his mother still does his laundry.

"Well, to admit weakness of any kind is a pride crusher, and staying sober takes a Higher Power's help, right?" I look for Jack's reaction over the top of my coffee cup before continuing. "That alone is more growth than many nonalcoholic people are willing to make."

"Oh, definitely." Ripping open three packets of real sugar, Jack empties them into his double espresso, stirs, and downs the whole cup at once—Italian style.

"What do you think about therapy? I mean, I know you have a degree in it, but not all psychologists partake of their own skills," he asks nonchalantly, brushing crumbs off the table and into his napkin. (Such a polite boy.)

"I went to therapy before I got my divorce, but instead of letting me talk about my screwed-up husband, she kept asking about my freaking father. One maniac at a time, please."

He laughs. "Those sons-a-bitchin' shrinks have the gall to suggest that our parents might be connected to our other problems? Go figure …"

Jack's teeth are very straight and white. I shake my head.

"What?" he asks.

"So much insight coming from a *man*." I laugh.

"Ah, man-hater warning received. Well, just so you know, I've been at the ranch avoiding all of you conniving wenches as well. Truce?"

We shake hands.

"I suppose someday I'll do a fourth step," I mumble.

"Always a good idea."

"Who are you, my sponsor?" I snap.

"Did I just hear a mental door slam?"

"You aren't the only one with issues. Let's go." I gather my purse and head for the door, aware that he is probably checking out my butt.

"By the way, you look pretty today," he says.

THIRTY-FIVE

"I'M IN EXTREME PERIL."

"Afraid, afraid, afraid."

"I know, Oz-God. Don't rub it in."

"That's not what I mean."

"What, then?"

"I was watching the fear chemicals pump through your brain."

"My father's bimbo wife called me this afternoon and said he was at death's door."

"Does that make you afraid?"

"She said he wants me to know he loves me. What a crock. Couldn't he tell me himself? I can't even *begin* to tell you how little I care."

"I have an idea. Let's play a guessing game."

"I hate your games."

"How was your date with Jack?"

"Not a date: bank … coffee … room full of drunks."

"Monosyllables, eh?"

"This is a trap."

"Wrong."

"Jack said I looked pretty."

"The nerve of that boy!"

"First men find me attractive, and then they want in my pants. Why did he have to ruin everything?"

"Here's a neural pathway we can follow."

"You can't make me."

"What if a woman compliments you? Does she want in your pants?"

"If a woman says I'm pretty, the pathway takes a different fork toward a dark and complex place full of envy and competition—female detritus."

"Yours or theirs?"

"Please stop."

"What do you think other women see when they look at you?"

"No one should be threatened by me! When I'm not in the classroom, I look like crap. I don't even brush my hair on the weekend, just wind it up any which way. I'm divorced and have been arrested, for Pete's sake."

"And you don't see how that could be threatening?"

"I guess if someone were a religious rule follower all her life, I may represent what she was told to avoid—the little rebel/slut that could and did."

"Is that all?"

"Maybe a *bad girl* like me might try to steal her husband ... I've never really thought about it."

"Most people are afraid of being judged. They might see those who are brave enough to break the rules as attractive."

"Is my father really dying?"

"What are you feeling?"

"I can't think about him without wanting to drink or throw up. Please let me run away from this."

"Where do those memories take you?"

"They lead to ... Wait—I remember—something."

"Can you tell me?"

"Nooo ... so much shame! I don't want to go back there. Reliving this will destroy everything!"

"I will protect your heart."

"Do you promise?"

"Yes."

"It was Easter, I think. Yes, because my dress was white and frilly with a yellow satin ribbon tied around the middle ... the most beautiful dress I'd ever owned. I wore a white hat with yellow flowers and had little white gloves."

"So precious."

"The gloves were amazing—my hands looked so clean. I wouldn't take them off, even when the Sunday school teacher gave us chocolate eggs to eat."

"Keep going. I'm right here."

"An old, busty woman sat in the front pew every Sunday. She had a huge mole with a long hair growing out of it."

"Really?"

"I may be imagining the hair. Anyway, she saw me with chocolate all over my clothes. I will never forget the look of disgust that distorted her face. 'What a dirty little girl you are,' she said. 'Look, you've ruined your outfit, even your socks. You should be ashamed!'"

"She basically cursed you."

"When I looked down at the brown smears on my clothes, I knew I was ruined forever, covered with a filth I could never wash off. I burst into tears and ran outside to hide, leaving a trail of dirty gloves, hat, shoes, and socks."

"And why did getting chocolate on your dress cause a lifetime of ruin?"

"My father had bought me the magical Easter outfit the day after he first molested me."

"Go on."

"I can't! I couldn't stop him. I was so small and weak. I would just freeze in the dark … go dead inside until it was over."

"My heart is bleeding."

"What does it matter now? He's dying, and I'm glad."

"That day a horrendous lie became truth for you."

"Which lie? That cops don't protect you, church is not a loving place, and I don't deserve anything lovely or valuable because I'm filthy? No biggie. I'm used to it now."

"Those lies are still tearing your life apart."

"I don't want to play this game anymore."

"Intellectualizing pain is easier for you?"

"If intellectual means brainy, profound, gifted, talented, academic, educated, knowledgeable, genius? You bet."

"Better than the alternative, right?"

"I want to matter, to be admired, and to have the right answers to every question so people will think I'm smart and worthy. I crave affirmation from basically everyone I meet. It's so hideously needy. If I don't get what I crave, I look for ways to reject *them*."

"What would mattering look like?"

"What do you mean?"

"You already have a PhD. No one in your family even went to college. Do you want to be rich? Marry a good man and have children? Publish a book? Find inner peace?"

"I don't have to worry about any of that. I'll never have those things because I'm chemically addicted to self-loathing."

THIRTY-SIX

"**G**OOD MORNING?"

"Maybe in your dimension …"

"*I see.*"

"Last night I dreamed about helping my childhood friend plunge a ton of crap out of her toilet."

"*Where would the world be without plumbers?*"

"Dig a hole; cover it up. Dig a hole …"

"*It's probably going to take supernatural help to unclog your life.*"

"You make a plunger sound like Excalibur."

"*Only the chosen can wield that holy weapon.*"

"Yesterday, my aha moment turned into a royal migraine. All systems shut down except one—I vomited all night—flushed it down."

"*Buh bye!*"

"I've decided that a tolerable life is enough for me."

"*You don't want the whole enchilada?*"

"I'm afraid of men, of love, and of life itself. I don't need any of it. There, I said it."

"*You aren't going to comment on my association between men and enchiladas?*"

"I know I can't help craving spicy food, but I've learned my lesson. The cheese makes me fat, and then the enchiladas don't find me attractive anymore, have an affair, and leave me for some other taco."

"*What about Jack?*"

"Jack is scary because he makes me hope again."

"Interesting choice of words."

"Stop it! Why does every single person make comments about my stupid name?"

"It's a plot ..."

"Tell me this, what about children who *weren't* abused? What if their parents slathered them in love and encouragement?"

"That too becomes hardwired."

"Talk about playing favorites ..."

"I told you—no one escapes the lessons. There are plenty of other enticing experiences that plague humans: criticism, gossip, self-righteousness, vanity, false humility, pride, greed, lust, entitlement ..."

"We alcoholics are just more out front with our powerlessness. Is that what you mean?"

"Pride can kill relationships just as easily as alcohol."

"Are you kidding? So I should be grateful? What if someone grows up in a good Christian home with no obvious addictions, goes to church, looks good on the outside, but is hiding his or her sins?"

"What has been your experience with that?"

"They point fingers at the rest of us, making a big deal out of the rules we are breaking that qualify us for ejection from their salvation club."

"You would never point fingers or judge anyone else ..."

"At least I'm not afraid to be miserable."

"Angst is your art form."

"May I print that on a T-shirt?"

"Depression, pain, and guilt are the bits of clay that you consistently choose to work with."

"Your point?"

"You know how to push and smooth the suffering until it takes shape and becomes something beautiful."

"Uh ... Things aren't so smooth from down here. My handmade pity pots are all shattered."

"I'll get the Gorilla glue."

THIRTY-SEVEN

"CAN YOU HEAR THAT?" MICAH HESITATES, HOLDING HIS melting ice cream sandwich in midair.

Dula looks at her brother and her eyes light up. "Look! The big white Suburban! Hurry, Miss Hope—Miss Nellie is comin'!" Dula grabs my hand, pulling me out of the porch swing.

Nell Lister-Findley gets out of her sparkling SUV and takes off her cowboy hat, fluffing her hair. She looks spiffy in turquoise cowboy boots, jeans, and an elaborately embroidered Mexican shirt. I want to be her when I grow up—wealthy, happily married, and all her ducks in a row.

The kids swarm her, both talking at once and making it difficult for her to walk. I feel no envy, at least not in the "old" way, only the desire to know her better—a new feeling, for sure.

Nell, the children, and I carry plates of cold fried chicken and potato salad out by the pool. Earlier, I had helped Marcella squeeze fourteen lemons and stir tons of sugar into the lemonade—best I've ever had.

After lunch, Micah and Dula play around the pool, and Nell retrieves some pale pink nail polish from her shoulder bag. Marcella has gone back to her house for a nap.

"Hope, would you be offended if I paint my nails?" Nell asks.

"Of course not," I say, tempted to hide my neglected toes under a towel. Dula joins us with another chicken leg and no plate, plopping down on the end of Nell's chaise lounge.

"Here, Dula." I hand her my slightly used napkin, and she ineffectually tries to wipe the fried chicken particles off her face.

"Miss Nellie, can I tell her?"

Nell nods.

"Guess what, Miss Hope. Next Sunday, Micah and I are gonna get *baptized*!"

"You are?"

I am totally unclear about the correct response to this ritual.

Dula puts her foot up next to Nell's, and she begins painting the little girl's toenails. Dula is watching Nell so intently she can barely continue speaking.

"We were gonna do it a while back, but then Momma went to heaven, and Daddy wasn't ready to celebrate yet."

"Is there a party involved?" I feel stupid.

Dula stops and looks at me through squinted eyes ... the same way she listens for arrowheads.

After seeing Dula's intense expression, Nell shakes her head, pressing her lips together and focusing on the little girl's feet.

"Miss Hope?"

"Yes, Dula."

"You *have* been baptized, right?"

"Uh, I'm not sure ... maybe as a baby. My family didn't really go to church much."

Nell mutters to me, "There's no escaping now ..."

I'm not sure if Nell means Dula or me.

"But, Miss Hope ..." She pauses. "Didn't you ever want to tell the whole wide world that you belong to Jesus?"

("Not no, but *hell* no," I refrain from screaming at this sweet evangelist.)

"Well, Dula, here's the thing. If I get baptized, all my bridges to the secular world would burst into flames," I say.

Nell shouts with laughter.

"What does that mean?" Dula looks fragile. like she might cry.

"Never mind, sweetie. I'm just not ready like you are."

Dula's toes are finished, and she seems to accept my response, walking stiff-legged for a few steps before forgetting her wet toenail polish and running toward the house.

"You've got to watch that little one. She's an old soul." Nell slides her sunglasses down her nose and slaps the nail polish bottle on the palm of her hand. "Your turn," she says.

"Oh, no. My feet are awful."

Nell is already lifting my foot into her lap as if she and Dula are part of a dance team and it's Nell's turn to cut in. I brace myself.

"I'm sort of spiritual, you know," I say defensively. "I had this experience on the beach last year ... I guess you could call it religious." Sweat drips down my neck into my shirt.

"Did you know that you have the most gorgeous feet?" Nell is all but spreading my toes apart—looking at my heel and arch, and then she begins massaging.

(Didn't the woman hear what I said?)

She presses her thumbs into the ball of my foot, and I have to hold back a moan.

"When I was in college," Nell continues, "I gave all my sorority sisters foot rubs and pedicures. Don't ask me why—probably God's wicked sense of humor."

"Why do you say that?" I ask.

"You know, the whole wash-your-neighbor's-feet humility thing, except I wasn't humble by any definition."

I hold my breath.

"I went kinda berserk for about ten years," she admitted.

Shocked, I try to pull my foot loose, but her grip is strong.

"That surprises you?" she laughs and reaches for the other foot.

"I'm sorry. How rude of me. You just seem so ..."

"So ... what? Middle-aged goody-goody? Or a snobby rich girl?"

(I detect an issue lurking.)

"Oh my God, not at all. None of those things, in fact, you are the least ... person like that I've ever met."

"Really? Good. I'm grateful for the compliment."

Nell's foot massage is otherworldly.

"You know, I was a therapist—seems like a couple of lifetimes ago," she says.

(I'm positive she doesn't mean *lifetimes* the way I might—too soon for me to play *that* card.)

"Well that makes sense. No wonder you're so easy to talk to."

"I don't know." Nell says, brushing polish on my big toenail. "People sometimes treat you differently when they think you are analyzing them."

"Why would you be insecure about what anyone thinks about you?" I ask and then want to kick myself.

Nell is silent for a moment. "My daddy was a big rancher who wanted a son instead of a scrawny daughter. My mother loved me but had a very hard time showing it."

"Mine too," I say.

"In high school, Mama asked Daddy for a divorce, took half of his millions, and moved to South America."

"Nobody escapes the bullshit ... Oops!" I slam my hand over my mouth.

"That's for damn sure!"

"Sorry for cussing," I say.

"Shit, shit, shit. Does that make you feel better?" Nell smiles.

"Actually, yes. Please continue your story."

"Most of the men I dated just wanted to get close to my father's money, until Mort came along." Nell smiles and looks away. "I had a dangerous and destructive decade or two before I found him."

"Are you uncomfortable talking about those days?"

"Most of the time, yes." Nell turns her attention back to my feet, waiting for me to continue.

"I don't mean to be rude, but since I came to the ranch, I've been having a really rough time. It's so hard to find people, especially women, to talk to." My voice disappears in a squeak, and I stare at the ground, mortified.

"Hope, you wouldn't believe how far I've come. It has only been since Tamar—she's our daughter—completely rejected me and our wealthy Texas lifestyle and moved to New York City to work with the homeless that I really started to get in touch with some of the deep stuff from my past."

I sit quietly, listening … praying that she will continue.

"You know, I didn't ask to be born into money," Nell says, unable to make eye contact. "At first, everything in life seemed so random, like: Why wasn't I born a boy? Or, why Texas and not New York? Do you ever feel that way?"

I nod. "In my case, the questions were more like, why was I born at all? And, how long will I be forced to suffer?"

"Sometime I'd like to hear your story too." Nell smiles and quickly squeezes my hand.

"Someday," I say, still feeling shy.

Nell leans back on her chaise. "I don't know if this is something that just happens to people with money and influence or everyone. Oh, that sounds so snobby. I'm sorry. I hate talking about these things. All my life I've been treated with envy and judgment for simply being a Lister. I learned to hide everything—dress down, cuss like a sailor, and never reach for my true potential."

"Why? You had every resource, every opportunity laid at your feet?"

"Yes, few understand how the have-nots hate and resent those who have."

"I never thought about that side of the coin. In this country, it's almost like we're trained to believe everyone is entitled to what the wealthy have."

Nell continues. "As a child, I never realized how indoctrinated I was about proper etiquette and behavior, proper grammar, clothing, education … religious beliefs. I think there is even a chapter in *Miss Manners* on the hidden but *acceptable* way to screw up and rebel so you can maintain your country club membership!" We both laugh.

"Yours is a world I can't relate to, except the part about the indoctrination of dysfunctional beliefs … which, in my case, were obvious from the beginning."

"You're lucky to know that so young. I stumbled on that piece of enlightenment much later than you have."

"Broken and twisted is enlightenment? Who knew?" I say.

"It doesn't matter where, when, or to whom we are born … We are all broken."

"Is that what Miss Manners says?"

"No, Miss Manners teaches us how to fool each other into believing we aren't broken at all."

"How old are you?" The question escapes the safety of my mouth.

"I'll be sixty-two in July. How old are you, Hope?"

"In my thirties … I'm kind of a big mess right now. About a month ago I had an alcoholic relapse and then the snakebite … not to mention what's happening with Jack." I begin laughing at the absurdity of my sudden outburst of intimate revelations.

Nell blows on my pretty painted toenails and chuckles. "Oh, yes. Let's talk about you and Jack! Start from the beginning …"

THIRTY-EIGHT

RENDEZVOUS. WHAT A POOFY FRENCH WORD. WHO KNOWS WHAT this day will hold? I'm romanticizing this now moment because I want to. I wish every day could be this full of promise. Maybe my life would be transformed if I ceased obsessing over my own belly button … paralysis of analysis.

Here I go again, braving the outback like a Crocodile hunter. I'm not sure what happened to my snake hammer. Micah probably spray-painted it gold and made a trophy out of it. I need a machete or a real weapon. Fear no evil, trust God, and wear Kevlar!

The hand-drawn map Jack made leads me beside a small lake labeled "Eagle Tank." Jack told me that these huge watering holes were made for cattle and horses—dug in the 1800s by men with shovels and donkey-driven scrapers. Over the decades, trees have muscled their way around these water sources that today provide me with shade and seclusion. Thanks, Oz-God.

Do feral eyes track me as I sit like a statue, watching the wind tickle the top of the water? Does evil pace on bobcat feet, silent, sniffing for the blood of the weak? I don't want to live in fear anymore.

I wrote my father a letter and sent it with Manuel into town. Done deal, no takebacks or do-overs. I told my father that he had almost destroyed me and hurt me in ways that still poisoned my relationships with men. I may be new to the idea of forgiveness, but I'm trying to listen. I told my dad I forgave him in the best way I could and then signed my name—not very warm but hopefully a drop in the bucket. This process isn't a party.

From my brushy hideaway, I watch Jack approach. He looks down as if following my footprints … hunting me. (How delightfully primal.) I wonder what he thinks of me. I vaguely remember him sitting in my room after the snakebite. That seems so long ago. Am I falling for him? I fall for most men. Crap. I want this time to be different.

He stops where my tracks disappear into the grass and looks out over the water, probably worrying about how low it is. Jesus, this ranch needs rain. I scramble up the bank so he can see me. His wave is hesitant; he must be nervous too.

"I'm so glad you're here," I say, trying to catch my breath. "I've been thinking."

"Oh, really?"

"Yes, big shot. I think quite often." I sound sassy.

"Thinking gets me into trouble … especially when I think about you," he says with a slow smile.

I am stunned. He isn't even blushing.

"Way to knock me off balance, cowboy!"

"I figured a preemptive strike might work to my advantage."

"Mission accomplished. I forgot what I was going to say."

"You were thinking?" he says.

"Oh, yeah. Everything seems clearer out here in the boonies. You've lived on the ranch your whole life; you must know what I mean."

A flicker of irritation crosses his face. "Except for all those years I was studying, traveling, and making something of myself."

"I didn't mean to imply you were a hick or …"

"No, it's my fault. I'm so defensive about people's assumptions that I snap at everyone. Pretty easy to see the chip on my shoulder, eh?" He touches my arm. "Now what is your profound revelation?"

"Sometimes my words get tangled up."

"Ya think? That's no revelation." he says. I take a swipe, but he gracefully deflects my hand and twirls me around in front of him until both of us are looking out over the water. I blow out a breath and continue.

"For weeks I've been almost obsessed with thoughts about life, death, and spirituality, and then *this* happens."

"*This*?" he says.

"Yeah, what you and I are doing."

"As far as I can tell, we aren't *doing* anything," he jokes.

"Everything on the ranch feels so wild and free. The raw power scares me, and so do you."

"I guess I don't think about it—the ranch, I mean. I've always moved at this pace, watching for animals, paying attention to the weather, working hard ..."

Without thinking, Jack starts massaging my shoulders as he talks. It feels way too good. I find an excuse to bend down and move away from him.

"Look at this dung beetle," I say, reaching for a branch covered with tiny orange puffballs to help me regain balance. I can almost hear Oz-God laughing. "What smells so delicious? ... Ouch! Those little fuzzy buggers have thorns in them!"

A drop of blood appears on my index finger. Jack snaps off a small sprig from the tree and sniffs deeply before handing it carefully to me. "If my senses are correct," he says, lifting his nose to the wind like a hound, "the desert scent today is dusty huisache and white brush with a dash of pond scum."

"Yum, delicious. Look, you're bleeding too." Impulsively, I take Jack's hand and press my bleeding fingertip to his thumb. "There. Now we are blood related. You better not have some deadly disease."

Jack pops his finger into his mouth. "Back atcha."

"Did you know I spent some time on an ashram in India after my father died?" He glances at me, gauging my reaction to the rapid subject change.

"No way! I've always wanted to do that!"

"Yeah, I studied meditation, the guru-mantra type ... Never really *got it*. I was always too focused on what I was or wasn't supposed to see after my mind became still, which it never did."

I'm listening so intently that I don't notice our faces are very close. Jack chuckles and backs up—his turn to take some space.

"They told me that every moment contains a possible universe, and it freaked me out." He picks up a rock to throw. "By the way, my dad was a drunk ... Did I already tell you that?"

I nod, forcing myself to stay silent and let him jump from subject to subject.

"Uncle Mick was the oldest and ran the ranch—handling the business end of things. I think people assumed that his wild-ass brother was sleeping with the help, and I was a product of that."

Jack throws another rock, and it skips four or five times.

"Where is your mother from?" I ask.

"Monterrey, Mexico—her family also owns a lot of land, but my mother was a rebel and refused to be married against her will. She packed her bags and had a friend drive her to Laredo."

"Where she met your father?"

"She probably married him too fast and for the wrong reasons, but there it is. I've tried so hard to get past my father's wasted life."

"Believe me, I know—sins of the father and all that."

"I think my anger habit is harder to break than anything else. But we don't have to talk about it anymore." Jack looks toward the east, his face full of concern. "Look at the sky," he says.

I glance at the clouds. "You do know that I'm over thirty, don't you? Just in case you thought I was just a cute, young thing."

"I know how old you are—checked your W-2." He smiles. "I've got you beat by a year and a half. Besides, you look great, even if you are old."

I stare at Jack's mouth, wondering how it would feel for him to kiss all my bad memories away. Is this how it starts? Using a man to fix my feelings of unworthiness? Why can't I stop analyzing?

Pulling his eyes from my face, he checks the sky again. "The wind is really picking up."

A huge bank of clouds has changed from purple to greenish and seems to be churning.

"This isn't good," he says. "We better get to my truck. I think we can still beat the storm."

Turning my face to the wind, my hair blows wildly behind me—exhilarating. Jack chases his Spurs cap into the bushes.

"Maybe we'll see some dust devils on the way back!" I shout.

Jack reaches for my hand. "If we don't hurry, we might see more than that!"

THIRTY-NINE

Jack is driving way too fast, but I don't care. Strong gusts of wind spank at the vegetation on the sides of the road—rocking the truck. The desert is coming to life—electric and terrifying. Every nerve in my body seems to be overstimulated and focused on survival.

I feel like laughing or screaming, and I can't explain it. I've never felt so alive. If I die today, snatched up by a tornado and flung over the rainbow, I will leave this earth happy—and be even more satisfied if I get to kiss this man before I go.

"This'll have to do." Jack turns the steering wheel sharply, leaving the road and following an overgrown path.

"Are we nearing your house?" The sky has turned almost black, and I am finally aware of the danger we are in.

"There's an abandoned adobe back here. I used it as a fort when I was a kid."

I'm having trouble breathing. "But we have to get to a real shelter! I've seen what tornados can do. We aren't safe out here. We—"

Jack slows down and grabs the back of my neck with his big hand, shifting his gaze back and forth between my face to the uneven road. Even with the noise and dust-filled wind swirling around us, he radiates strength.

"Hope, you're going to have to trust me. I will do everything in my power to protect you. God will do the rest."

His statement is simple, like butter on fresh bread.

"OK," I say, taking a deep breath.

The overgrown tracks dip down toward a dry wash, and I see the crumbling remains of a chimney rising behind some tall mesquite trees. The truck skids to a stop, and Jack forces his door open against the wind, dragging me across the seat. It feels as if my whole life has led to this moment.

When I look behind us, a surge of adrenaline shoots through my arms and legs. "Jack, *Jack*, look!"

"I know. It's a twister. Come on!"

Most of the roof to the small building has rotted away, and two whole walls are gone.

"Where are we going to hide? Is there a basement?" I shout.

Jack pulls me toward the huge fireplace.

"No, no, no! It will fall in on us—bury us alive!" Rigid with panic, I can't move.

Jack's mouth is moving, but the wind is too loud for me to hear him. His sheer strength pushes me into the four-by-four-foot opening. Folding his long legs in after me, he wraps his arms tightly around my chest, his back still partially exposed to the raging elements.

Like in an underground cavern, there is very little light. I hear a thud, and Jack grunts as something hits his back. I press farther into the hole, willing myself to become smaller so I can pull him in closer. Jesus, God, all you guys, protect us.

I can hear Jack's voice now, low and husky, praying right beside my ear. Melting against him, peace floods through me. We aren't alone.

Quite a few very cramped and sweaty minutes later, my brain kicks in—thinking about black widow spiders and how they love dark, abandoned fireplaces. At least my extremities are covered. My folded leg throbs, reminding me that I've already had my allotment of sharp fangs and venom for the month.

Although Jack's body completely blocks the fireplace opening, the sounds leaking in around him have changed from a roar to intermittent rumblings of thunder.

"Are we safe? Can we get out now?" Something is crawling down my collar; I try to move my arm enough to slap it.

"How do you like our date so far?" he whispers.

Jack sounds completely serious. I can't stop the laughter from rocking my body.

He is shaking too. "I want you to know how hard this was to plan." He wheezes and jerks back, trying to catch his breath, hitting his head on the top edge of the fireplace.

"Damn!" he says as soot, bat guano, and black widow egg sacs, crumble into our open mouths.

"That's it." I cough, sputter, and spit. "We're outta here." I brace my feet against the back wall and shove Jack out of the fireplace and onto his back, landing on top of him.

The wrathful wind has touched the earth and moved on, leaving only the storm behind. I sigh, no longer afraid.

Making no move to sit up, Jack puts his arm around me, and I rearrange, snuggling close to his warm, rain-drenched body. Grateful to be alive, we lie together in the mud, lifting our filthy faces to the glorious refreshing wetness.

"What are we going to do now?" I whisper, listening to the beat of Jack's heart.

"Well, at some point we're going to have to get out of these mucky clothes."

I try to jerk away, but he tightens his grip.

"Hold on there, sister." He sits up and scoots me up next to him, returning his arm to my shoulders. "I didn't mean it *that* way. We both need to take this thing slowly."

"This *thing*?" I say, feeling vulnerable.

"You know what, Hope?" Jack lifts my chin so I can't avoid his eyes. "You're in for a treat. After this kind of rain, the desert will bloom like crazy."

"I can't wait." I smile.

As Jack's lips move toward mine, I close my eyes and let my worries rest for a moment—welcoming the first rays of healing as they peek from behind the clouds.

EPILOGUE

"Hey, Oz–God, do you know what's weird?"

"Oh, yes. I know all the weird things. People are so afraid to talk about the supernatural ..."

"Wait, or I'll forget the profound things I want to report."

"I suppose our exploration of the world of the weird Universe can wait awhile."

"I think that I have always mixed spiritual stuff with my own abusive dad ... just projected it all onto the invisible powers of an all-knowing being as just another ruse to steal my soul."

"Like thinking that our purpose was the total domination of humans for our own twisted pleasure?"

"Exactly. I keep thinking about people I know who profess to be atheist. I wonder what their earthly fathers were like."

"Mothers and fathers are unwittingly responsible for helping create neural pathways that can lead to a lifetime of misunderstanding the love available in the spiritual world. Thus begins each human's journey back to his or her individual truth."

"But why does it work that way? Why is life so painful? Why aren't we smarter?"

"If the spiritual quest was easy, there would be no free will, no process, no sacrifice that leads to relationship and a new level of ascension."

"At least I'm done now ..."

"Oh my, Hope. You've just begun—no done about it."

"Don't you ever get sick of being a know-it-all?"

"Just take it one day, one moment, one prickly pear apple at a time."

"Kicking and screaming is my forte, you know. Just for future reference."

"Thanks for the heads-up."

"I'm not sure I can get out of the basement yet. Hey, do you want a pedicure? Nell taught me to give great ones."

"Might want to pass those on to people with feet."

"Do you want to know a scary secret?"

"Those are the best kind."

"I don't want our journey to end."

"Yours and Jack's?"

"No, whatever it is that I have with you."

"Did you feel that, my treasure?"

"What?"

"The earth moved …"

ENDORSEMENTS (for A Divine Scavenger Hunt)

"[*A Divine Scavenger Hunt*] … the overall drama is profound, stimulating, brilliant, sophisticated, tender, funny, heavy, light…and more than a little sneaky, artistically speaking, in the ways it touches the mind and the soul."

Dr. Earl Koile
Professor Emeritus of Educational Psychology
University of Texas, Austin, Texas

"*A Divine Scavenger Hunt* is a gutsy experiment in creating a conversation between God (Spirit) and a woman who has tried every depersonalized, non-god alternative…

Eugene Peterson
Translator of *The Message* Bible

"…do not open [*A Divine Scavenger Hunt*] at night if you have to work the next morning: you may not be able to put it down.

Rev. Dr. Susan Barnes, Director Emeritus
of the Dallas Museum of Art

"*A Divine Scavenger Hunt* is a bold breakthrough book. I strongly recommend this book for the cynical – or those already committed (to the spirit world.) Read it!"

Keith Miller
Best-selling author of *A Taste of New Wine*

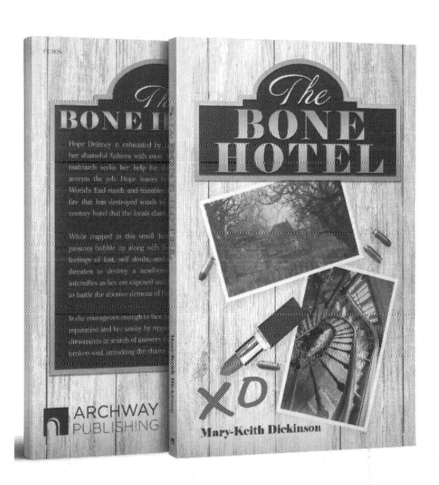

Marykeithdickinson.com

Printed in the United States
by Baker & Taylor Publisher Services